I0681279

Raven and Snow

SEEKING HIS FAMILIAR

SAMANTHA CAYTO

ENTWINED PUBLISHING

Seeking His Familiar
ISBN # 978-1-80250-620-4
©Copyright Samantha Cayto 2025
Cover Art by Kelly Martin ©Copyright December 2025
Interior text design by Entwined Publishing
Published by Eternal, an Entwined Publishing imprint

Published in 2025 by Entwined Publishing, United Kingdom.

Entwined Publishing is a division of Totally Entwined Group Limited.

Entwined Publishing books by Samantha Cayto

Single Books
One Night in a Dungeon
Man Candy
Against a Rising Tide
Safeword

Alien Slave Masters
The Captain's Pet
The Rebellious Pet
The Untamed Pet
The Captive Pet
The Inconvenient Pet
The Undercover Pet

Alien Blood Wars
Blood Dance
Dangerous Dance
Slave Dance
Star Dance
Mating Dance
Healing Dance
Smoke Dance
Final Dance: Part One
Final Dance: Part Two

Treaty Brides
Boi Bride
The Diplomat's Bride
Stolen Bride
The Substitute Bride
The Secret Bride
The Brigand's Bride
The Cordial Bride
The Desert Bride
The Siege Bride

Debt Slave
Bound to Him
Minding his Master
His Undercover Slave

Raven and Snow
Seeking His Familiar

Anthologies
Right Here, Right Now: Never the Groom

Collections
Rules of Summer: In the Heat of the Dungeon
Dark and Deadly: Dream Demon
S.W.A.L.K.: His True Heart
His Harem: Room for Elijah

SEEKING HIS FAMILIAR

Chapter One

"A snow leopard." James Byrne stared at the adorable familiar standing in front of him.

"Yes, indeed. Very rare. We are lucky to have acquired him."

Mr. Beatle, the headmaster of the Boston Academy for Familiars, oozed false charm. With his short, round physique and small squinty eyes, he even looked like the insect his name brought to mind. James kept his gaze on the boy, Aden. The familiar's coloring was unusual. His skin and almond-shaped eyes were tawny, while his hair hung in shaggy waves to his shoulders in a startling mix of black, red and gold. Despite his being housed in Boston, his family must have hailed from another country. He was dressed in the long smock that familiars were expected to wear to keep them from shredding their clothes when they shifted. The hem of the shapeless garment skimmed the tops of brown, leather slippers for modesty's sake.

Buying and selling familiars was perfectly acceptable, but God forbid someone catch sight of a well-turned ankle.

Mr. Beatle moved to stand next to his prize pupil. "His family has set a very dear price for him. I'm sure you'll agree that he's worth it."

When James had first arrived, the odious man had taken him in with one long sweep of his gaze and had judged him incapable of paying much. Not surprising. James' clothes were respectable but not costly. He preferred to put his generous settlement from the Boston police department to better use than dressing like a dandy. The bank draft he'd pulled from his pocket had convinced Beatle that James was a serious buyer.

James gave a nod. "I'll take him."

Beatle smiled with unbridled glee. "Excellent." He gave Aden a nudge forward. "He's all yours, Mr. Byrne."

The boy didn't so much as glance at him. In fact, he gave no outward sign of any emotion other than his fingers gripping a bit of his smock.

Poor thing is terrified. And why wouldn't he be? He was being sold like cattle, except, unlike such beasts, he knew what his future held in store for him. Or, at least, he thought he did. No doubt familiars had a healthy fear of being controlled by a witch. And, sadly, many witches were cruel to their familiars. With few laws against it, and even those not enforced very often, Aden had every reason to be afraid.

I will be good to him. It was the best he could do to ease his conscience. He needed a familiar or his fledgling business would be doomed to finding wayward pets and misplaced umbrellas. With Aden to boost his power, he could tackle the hard cases of finding people and valuable items rich people would pay handsomely to retrieve. His excitement over the prospect was hard to contain. He had to rein himself in, however. The first step was to bond with the familiar and that process made his stomach flutter with nerves. Lying with another man was not something he'd ever done, yet looking at his soon-to-be bed partner, he couldn't deny that he was going to enjoy it. His cock was already half-hard at the prospect.

"Thank you, Mr. Beatle." Civility forced him to extend his hand for a shake. He made short work of it. "Aden, fetch your things and we'll be off."

For the first time, the boy raised his gaze. "Sir?"

"He has nothing of his own to bring, Mr. Byrne." Beatle looked almost chagrined at his own statement. "His parents didn't leave anything with him. They even took the clothes he was wearing."

James knew that many parents resisted the mandated boarding of their familiar children. He'd been on a few roundup missions himself as a young copper. It had made him sick to his stomach to literally wrestle adolescent kids from their parents' arms. But familiars had always been given something of their home life to take with them. Toys and such. And he'd tried to hang back and remind the distraught parents that they could visit their children at the boarding school and that eventually they'd receive recompense. Not that the words had eased their pain, at least not in that moment.

He'd understood the grief of those people even as he accepted the wisdom of government control over creatures who could prove dangerous to the public. Older children who had not yet reached the wisdom and control of an adult were problematic enough without adding the ability to shift into vicious animals.

It was common sense to keep them locked up and monitored, as was binding the adult familiars to a witch to take over the obligation. Witches were good for society and, with the power boost of the familiars, that good became great. Everyone knew familiars were emotional and capricious beings. Their witch tamed them and gave them purpose. Still, he simply couldn't fathom anyone just abandoning their child, waiting a few years for their meager cut of the sale.

James resolved to buy the boy whatever he wanted, once the business took off. He'd pamper him. Yes, that's what he would do. Aden would have a happy life with him.

"I see. We'll be off, then." As he turned to leave, he placed a hand on Aden's shoulder.

The boy flinched and tensed for a moment but didn't resist being guided out of the room. The long hallway that led to the front doors held a line of familiars on each side. No one said anything. They merely watched James take Aden away in silence. It appeared to be some kind of ceremony, perhaps the boarding school's way of showing that there was an endgame to the children's lives in the dreary place. None of the familiars looked at them, though, or said anything. Like Aden, they kept their eyes down and their mouths shut. And yet, James felt a certain amount of condemnation emanating from those silent children.

James hardened his heart. Someone was always going to end up taking Aden, and he was damn glad to be that person.

The bright sun and fresh air outdoors lightened his mood. He took in a deep breath and jogged down the brick stairs. He moved his hand to grip the boy's arm to make sure he didn't trip. Aden had to raise his hem, like a woman would her skirts, as they went. As practical as the smocks were, he resolved to buy Aden a decent suit to wear when they weren't working. Dressed up, the boy would be a beauty. James wanted to give him as normal a life as possible, too. The smock proclaimed him a familiar and, even though Aden would be permitted to go anywhere so long as James was by his side, James hoped Aden would prove to be trustworthy enough to venture out on his own from time to time. It was only right after being cooped up in that old, gloomy boarding school.

His pride and joy was right where he'd left it. The shiny new paint glistened in the sunlight. Aden uttered something that sounded like awe at the sight of it. This was the first real response from the boy yet.

James beamed as he swept his hand toward the automobile. "It's a beauty, isn't it? An Oldsmobile Curved Dash, fresh off the assembly line." It had cost a pretty penny, too, but he didn't see it as an indulgence. A seeker witch needed to be able to get around quickly. Horse-drawn vehicles would soon be a thing of the past, he was sure of it, and he'd have the advantage over his competitors by already possessing the new invention once the demand picked up.

Aden's eyes were wide as he blinked up at him. "May I ask a question, sir?"

James was taken by surprise. He supposed familiars were taught to be seen and not heard, obedient to a fault. Well, that was not how he intended to run their relationship.

"You may ask me a question any time you like, Aden. And call me James. I may be your master in the eyes of the law, but I think of us as being more like partners."

Aden's expression relayed his skepticism on that point, but he didn't call James out on it. Instead he showed a delightful curiosity.

"How does it work?"

James smiled. "Get up on the seat and I'll show you."

He helped the boy up on the passenger's side of the bench, then went over to the driver's side. After setting the gearshift, he cranked the shaft. The engine came to life with a roar on the first try. James hopped up next to Aden. The seat was sufficiently wide for two people, unless one of them was as big as James. His thigh pressed against the familiar's. The contact sent a tingle straight to his groin, nearly making him groan. They'd be home soon enough and the growing need in him would be sated.

He slipped goggles onto his head, and he'd had the good sense to buy a second pair for Aden. He ignored Aden's flinch as he helped him put them on. It was obvious that the familiar's training had made him wary of being touched. Knowing that caused a ball of fury to form in his gut. He pushed it down with hard-fought control. His temper had always been a problem. It was important to keep it on a tight leash.

Taking off, he let the thrill of wind in his face ease his anger. As always, he enjoyed the staring and pointing that his relatively rare mode of transportation elicited from the pedestrians on the streets. He maneuvered around horses and carriages with a skill that improved with each outing. He wasn't as afraid of hitting anyone as he'd been the first few journeys. Still, there were a few angry shouts and waving fists from riders and drivers. Not everyone embraced innovation as much as he did. Most couldn't afford it even when they did. He was damn lucky to have been able to squeeze so much money out of the city, even though the reason for it continued to prick his anger. It was water under the bridge, as his mother would say, so he shoved those feelings aside and reveled in his new life of near luxury.

That included his apartment. It took a while, but when he finally was able to pull into the alley beside the building where he lived, he was excited to show Aden his new home. He hopped out of his automobile, careful to take the crank shaft and goggles with him. Then he helped Aden down and removed the goggles from the boy's face, pink from the wind.

"How did you like it?"

A smile flashed before the familiar answered. "It was fun."

"Yes, it was, and we're going to have more while we work."

Aden's expression shuttered again. "Yes, sir."

"James," he corrected, not unkindly.

"James."

Aden said nothing more as James led him around to the front of the building and up the stairs. "This used to be the home of a wealthy family. They've fallen on hard times since the crash and converted it into apartments, but not before they were able to add modern improvements."

He opened the front door and headed up the stairs, making sure that Aden followed. The foyer was somewhat shabby and his apartment was at the very top floor, but still, he was proud. A descendent of Irish immigrants, being able to move out of South Boston to the South End was an achievement. Even though the neighborhood was becoming more populated with other types of immigrants, it remained a place where old Boston families lived and was closer to his new office in the Back Bay.

James unlocked his apartment and stepped aside to usher Aden in. "It's only one room, but I have a kitchen area over there and, even better, a bathroom."

He gestured toward the room with a flourish. It was spectacular in that it contained a sink with running water, a claw-foot tub and a flushable toilet. Like his Oldsmobile, his indoor plumbing was on the vanguard of modern living. Enough sun showed through the windows that he didn't have to turn on a light but couldn't wait to show Aden that they had electric ones, not gas. He hoped the familiar would be impressed with his new home.

Aden didn't disappoint. The boy ogled his surroundings. "It's amazing."

James cleared his suddenly clogged throat. "I'm glad you think so. I want you to be happy here. With me." Suddenly shy, he feared his cheeks were flushing. "We need to bond, Aden. It's dangerous for you to be outside the Academy without being bonded."

Aden's gaze dropped. "I understand."

"I'll be careful with you." He took a step forward and carded his fingers through the boy's hair. It was like multi-colored silk.

Aden trembled a little at the touch, although he made no effort to avoid it.

James stepped back. "First, I want to see you in your animal form. I'm sure you're as beautiful as you are in your human skin."

His palms felt clammy as he watched Aden tug the smock open and let it fall to the floor. James caught a flash of a lean, smooth body and a slender cock before a sleek snow leopard stepped free of cloth and slippers. It stood staring up at him with Aden's tawny eyes. The mere sight of the animal caused James' witch senses to tingle with excitement. The power would grow once

14

he'd bonded with the familiar and the need for it spurred him into action.

"Change back and come lie face down on the bed."

Even as he gave the order, he whirled around to yank the covers off. Aden changed as he walked. It was magnificent how he went from fur to flesh in a graceful blur that left him a boy again. And one that crawled onto the bed and lay down as ordered. Aden wrapped his arms around the pillow and closed his eyes. His thin body shivered and his breathing became harsh.

"I won't hurt you." James wanted to soothe the boy's fear even though he wasn't sure he could make good on his promise.

When he'd gone to the Academy, he'd thought he would find a girl. His experience with women wasn't vast because he refused to use prostitutes. Yet, he was fairly confident in his skill with them. He had no experience with other men. What he and Aden were about to do would be illegal if they weren't a witch and a familiar. One more rationalization by society about what was acceptable. If a male familiar boosted the power of a male witch, well then everyone benefited, even if sodomy was an abomination before God. To him, it was a ridiculous way of thinking, although of course he'd given up on church a long time ago for a lot more reasons. The law hadn't mattered all that much to him because he'd never been attracted to other men. But Aden's small, firm buttocks were as fetching to him in that moment as any woman's pussy had been.

He nearly tore off his jacket in his sudden haste. His fingers grew clumsy as he worked the buttons of his waistcoat, shirt, then trousers. His dick sprang out from his underclothes before he removed them. Once he was completely nude, he breathed hard, as if he'd run a mile. The urge to sink himself into the familiar was almost overwhelming. He forced himself to slow down, take the time to do it right. From what he'd heard, Aden would need some preparation to be able to take him without too much pain.

He'd stashed a jar of petroleum jelly in his nightstand. He took it out and dipped two fingers in the greasy stuff. Then he knelt on the bed and put his clean hand on the small of Aden's back.

"Try to relax."

It was a pointless suggestion. Every muscle in the boy's body was tight, the cheeks of his buttocks no less so. He pried them apart as best he could to slip his lubricated fingers between them. The puckered ring of the familiar's hole was right where he'd expected. When he pushed against it, he was met with resistance. So, he tried massaging it with the pads of his fingers while also rubbing the small of the boy's back in slow circles.

"Relax, sweetheart. Let me in."

James' words were met with silence, although Aden's fingers dug into the pillow. After a minute of effort, he accepted that the boy was simply not going to be able to do as he asked. The bonding was going to be more difficult than he'd hoped. Perhaps the kindest thing was to be quick about it. He pushed past the resistance to thrust his fingers into the boy's ass. With a whimper, Aden jerked up. James pressed him flat again with his palm.

"Easy, now. It's going to be all right. And once we're past this first time, the bond between us will be wonderful."

That's what he'd heard, what he'd been assured of every time someone had worked to convince him to take on a familiar. It hadn't seemed important because he'd been living his life just fine with a little power and the human brains and brawn he'd been born with. Now that his livelihood depended on a bonding, he hoped the tales hadn't been exaggerated.

He thrust his fingers in and out slowly to loosen Aden's channel. When he encountered what he assumed must be the boy's prostate, he rubbed against it. His reward was a brief moan passing Aden's lips. But no amount of effort was making the intrusion any easier. He removed his fingers in order to gather more jelly to grease his cock. It was so hard and his balls were hugged so tightly to his body, he feared he'd spend before he managed to breach Aden's hole.

James kneed between the boy's legs, spreading them as much as he could, then lifted him by the hips for better access. He wanted to go slowly and carefully, but his growing need and the belief that no amount of effort was going to make this better for the familiar caused him to surge forward. He slid his cock between the quivering ass cheeks, found the hole with the tip of his shaft and shoved it in with one, hard thrust.

Aden cried out into the pillow and his hole squeezed tightly. He bucked against James' hold, but he was no match for James' strength. James wrapped an arm around the boy's waist to lift him higher and hug him closer. With one palm flat on the bed to brace himself, James fucked his familiar with short, hard strokes. He came within seconds with a blinding pleasure that had him throwing his head back. A groan unlike any he'd uttered before filled the room and he dug his fingers into the boy's soft flesh, reveling in the feel of the beauty that now belonged to him. The exhilaration of the usual sexual climax was short-lived. In its place bloomed something extraordinary.

Power.

Chapter Two

Aden lay with his face pressed against the pillow and his ass held high by the witch's strong hands. He couldn't help the trembling. It was all too much. It wasn't merely the pain of being breached, although that lingered along with a surprising hint of pleasure. The sensation of having his witch inside him, not only in his ass but in every piece of him, every corner of his body was frightening. This was what he'd been taught in the horrid place they'd called a school but had really been a prison. *Your witch will claim you, mind, body and soul.* They'd said he would no longer be in control of himself and should be happy for it. He'd never have to make a decision or worry about his future. His witch would rule over him for the rest of their lives.

Except as he waited for he didn't know what, it didn't feel exactly that way. He felt pretty much as he always had. If his witch had taken over his mind, he couldn't detect it. There was something there, however. Something...wonderful. For the first time in his life, he felt connected to another person instead of being separate and alone. It made him…happy, maybe? Perhaps it was only relief. This big, handsome man who'd bought him and now impaled him seemed nice, and he'd certainly matched every fantasy Aden had ever had about a man claiming him. When he touched Aden, it was gentle. No slaps. No hair-pulling. And he smiled. A lot. His white teeth gleaming and his eyes sparkling. Of course, Aden had been careful not to do anything to anger the man. He'd slip up eventually. He always did. Those big hands could send him flying across the room with one brutal blow if the witch was so inclined. Aden would do well to remember that.

He squirmed, couldn't help doing it, against the discomfort. Instead of admonishing him to stay still, the witch eased him down and slowly removed his giant cock. At least the thing felt that big. It had nearly split Aden in two. When he'd dared to wish that he'd be bonded with a male witch, his imagination had fallen short on what it would actually feel like to have a man shove his way inside his body. He had to believe it would get better with practice. His witch's next words gave him hope.

"Sorry, sweetheart. I guess the first time is rough. I'll work on making it better for you."

The witch gently pulled Aden's ass cheeks apart.

"There's no blood, thank God, but I bet you're sore. I'll draw you a bath."

The soft, comfy mattress bounced as the man got off. As he padded to the bathroom, Aden opened his eyes to get his first real look. Now, he could see that the man's large frame was all thickly layered muscle. With such a big, hard ass, it was no wonder he'd been able to pound into Aden so strongly. And the thing, still half hard, that dangled between his thick thighs wasn't as big as Aden had imagined it to be, although plenty big enough compared to other men he'd seen in the Academy's showers.

He shivered at the sight and his own meager cock stirred in a surprising way. Maybe their continued bonding would indeed prove pleasurable to some degree. He squeezed his ass. The witch had said no blood, and that was a relief, yet something dribbled past his hole and cooled against his inner thighs. He knew what it was. Part of his training involved a detailed account of what bonding meant. He'd been warned it would hurt, and it had. But no one had said it might feel good in some way. As he listened to the sound of water flowing, Aden thought it just might. At least with this particular witch. It didn't hurt, either, that he was a man of means. A tub inside an apartment was only for the rich, he'd been told. If he were good, he might find himself being indulged with all kinds of luxury.

The witch returned and scooped up Aden as if he weighed nothing and cradled him in his arms to return to the bathroom. Aden clung to the man's firm shoulders, surprised to find the skin smooth and nearly hairless. He was a little embarrassed at the coddling. His experience with being pampered was nonexistent because his parents were cold, distant people, as if they could sense what he was even before his first shift at thirteen. He'd known, of course. The animal that was part of him had lurked beneath his skin, ready to come out when Aden's human half was able to let it. He'd been packed off to the Academy the very next day. Even after five years, he could still remember his parents' grim expressions and how they'd shoved him away—literally—when he'd begged them to take him home again.

His life had changed, however. The witch lowered him into the steaming bath as if he were a young child. The experience would have been perfect but for the sting of the hot water on his abused hole. Aden couldn't hold back the wince.

The witch carded Aden's hair away from his face. "It hurts, huh?"

"A…a little." *Never complain. No one cares about your silly problems. Be grateful for what you have.* "It's fine," he added and sank down up to his chin.

The witch stared at him with a slight frown. "Hmm. Take as long as you like. I'll put together some lunch for us."

Aden sat straight, sloshing water dangerously close to the rim. "Um, I should do that." *Sir.* He was careful not to use the honorific, but there was no chance he'd call his witch by his first name. Servility and respect had been beaten into him.

The witch's frown deepened. "You're my familiar, Aden, not my servant. We'll take turns with the cooking, and I have a woman come in once a week to clean. My clothes go to the laundress, too. Our work as detectives is the most important thing for us to put our energies into. I'm only throwing some sandwiches together, anyway. Come out when you're ready."

With a grin and a quick pat on the head, the witch left Aden to soak away the stiffness that had come not only from the bonding but also from his tensing under the scrutiny of the man who was buying him, not to mention the fast ride in that motorcar. It didn't take long before he was almost asleep from the soothing warmth. As the water cooled, however, he forced himself to wash. The witch's soap had a soft, citrusy scent. It reminded him of the man himself. He supposed it made sense for them to smell alike.

A large towel waited for him. He quickly dried off, then dithered over whether he should pull the plug in the tub. It made no sense for the witch to want to bathe in his dirty water and with the flowing tap, it would be easy to fill again. Still, the safest course of action was to leave it alone. Back in the main room, he found his smock lying across the bed. He was mortified to realize he'd dropped it to the floor when the witch had made him shift. It was important he take care of his own things, which meant at the moment, his smock and leather-soled slippers.

He made short work of dressing and walked the few steps it took to join the witch where he sat at a small table by the far window. The man was taking big bites out of a thick sandwich while reading through some papers. Aden went to stand beside him, waiting for orders of what to do next.

The witch glanced at him. "Have a seat and eat your sandwich. It's only ham and cheese. And there's more water in the pitcher." He frowned again, an expression that seemed frequent. "You don't have to wait for permission, you know. This is your home. Help yourself to whatever you want, whenever you want."

Aden wasn't sure how to respond to that unexpected boon. "Thank you." Pulling out the chair opposite the witch, he sat, managing to hide how it stung when his ass hit the wood. He hoped he'd get used to the sex so that the discomfort would go away. He picked up his sandwich. It wasn't as thick as the witch's but it was enough for him. The first bite told him he was hungry, so he took another in quick succession.

"You're going to have to get used to calling me by my name, you know." The witch put down the papers and looked at Aden with raised eyebrows.

Aden froze, crushing the sandwich he held with his fingers, then managed to swallow his mouthful. "Yes…" He couldn't bring himself to say the man's name. It was ingrained to be respectful and hard to shove aside years' worth of training.

Always remember that your witch is your master or mistress. You are not equals. They have the power and your duty is to enhance it. Otherwise there's no point to your existence.

The witch leaned into the table. "James. Go on, you can do it."

Aden swallowed again with a dry mouth. "*James.*" It wasn't all that hard, after all, especially when his witch beamed at him.

"There you go." The man sat back. "As soon as you finish, I'm taking you to my tailor."

In the middle of a bite, Aden could only stare wide-eyed.

The witch—James—held up his palms. "I know, I know. Everyone thinks familiars should be clothed only in smocks. I find the whole thing ridiculous. When we're out in the field, it will be important for you to be able to shift in an instant. Otherwise, though, you should look as smart as any other man. It won't be anything fancy, mind. As soon as business picks up, we can both get better ones."

Aden nodded and hurried to finish his meal. He cleared the table without being asked and set the dishes in the soapstone sink. They'd keep until later. His witch, *James*, seemed keen to get going. So he hurried out of the door behind him.

* * * *

When James didn't take the automobile crank with them, Aden understood they'd be walking to wherever they were going. In the late afternoon, the sidewalks and roads were bustling with people, horses and carts. Sounds and smells assaulted him from all angles. His experience being in the Academy left him anxious out among humans. He didn't miss, either, the stares and smirks shot his way. He stuck close to James' side and was pathetically grateful when the man took his hand.

"Don't mind them. They're just jealous."

"Jealous?" Aden was startled enough by the statement to question it.

James tugged him around a street cart. "That's right. We have something special that they don't. It's easier for them to act as if we're weird than to admit their own envy."

Aden wasn't convinced that was true, but he had no chance to ask anything further because James turned to steps leading down to a basement store. A little bell over the door announced their arrival. It was a tailor's shop, mounds of fabric sitting on long shelves. A small, thin man with a shock of white hair came out of the back room.

The man sketched a short bow. "Good afternoon, Mr. Byrne."

"Good afternoon to you, Mr. Friedman." James pulled Aden forward. "This is my new familiar, Aden. He needs to be fully outfitted as a proper gentleman, if you please."

If the tailor thought the request odd, he didn't betray his thoughts in his expression. He simply nodded and ushered them into the back. Once there, he handed Aden a white union suit and gestured toward a curtain.

"If the young gentleman would kindly change, I'll do the measurements." He turned to James. "In the meantime, shall we pick out fabric?"

Smart man, he was deferring to James to make the decisions, which was only right. Aden wouldn't know what to pick anyway, never having made any decisions in his life about what he wore. As he stripped out of the smock and into the underclothes, he could hear the man talking. Something about green to bring out the color of his eyes, whatever that meant. There was talk about how with the summer months coming, linen made more sense. They'd be back for wool in the fall. Murmuring filtered through about stripes versus no stripes, the style of a waistcoat and how they had to factor in new shoes, something that Mr. Friedman could obtain once his size was known. Aden waited awkwardly in his union suit and leather slippers for the men to return.

Mr. Friedman scrutinized him. "Just as I thought. A slender lad." He glanced at James. "Have a care with him."

If James was startled by the remark, he didn't show it. "Always." He shot Aden a smile.

It was easy to relax then, the warmth of James' expression giving him comfort. He stood in all the poses the tailor demanded while he measured seemingly every part of him. The man wrote it all down in a notebook. Scribbled some more, then showed the piece of paper to James.

"I'll take full payment now for the union suit and half for the rest. It will be done within the week."

Aden was curious about the cost, feeling guilty. He couldn't imagine when and where he would don the clothing instead of his smock. But whatever the price, James merely took out a few bills from his pocket and handed them over.

He gestured toward the curtain. "Change back into your smock. The barber is next."

Aden couldn't help running his fingers through the long strands. He hadn't had short hair since entering the Academy. Longer hair was fitting for boy familiars. It marked them as such, much like the smock did. He wondered if he should explain it to James. Perhaps his witch didn't understand how things were done. Then again, who was he to question his witch?

Feeling more like himself back in his smock, he folded the union suit and carried it to the front of the shop. Mr. Friedman wrapped it in paper and tied the package with string. Soon, Aden was back on the street, being led by his witch to the barber.

* * * *

James wondered if it was normal to enjoy the feel of Aden's small hand slipped inside his larger one, whether he should be aroused simply by having the boy tucked against his side. It surprised him how amazing it had felt to sink himself inside the familiar for the purpose of bonding. He'd expected the activity to be a type of chore, albeit a pleasurable one. Sex was always thus, at least for him. He knew it could be that women often didn't enjoy it, and that was on the man, to his way of thinking. It took time to bring a woman to climax and selfish men made terrible lovers. He supposed the same was true for when it was two men. The one on the receiving end had to be treated with care. He knew he'd fallen down on that score. His bonding effort had been clumsy, giving Aden no pleasure. James would have to learn to do better. After all, they were going to be together for the rest of their lives.

The barber was just finishing up with a customer when they entered his shop. "Good afternoon, Mr. Haddad. Do you have time for another?"

The relatively young man grinned at him while he swept hair from his customer's collar. "Mr. Byrne. It's too soon for you to come. Your hair is perfect still."

Mr. Haddad took his efforts very seriously. James ran a quick hand over his slicked-back hair. Now that he worked for himself, he could wear it any way he wanted. His thick, wavy hair required a firm hand to keep it from going wild.

"It is indeed, Mr. Haddad. I'm here for my new familiar to benefit from your clever scissors."

The barber furrowed his brows as he accepted payment and ushered his other customer out of the door. Then he turned to stare at Aden as a sculptor might a piece of clay. It could have been James' imagination, but he felt the familiar press closer to him.

He squeezed the boy's hand and was about to say he wanted something short and neat such as his own. Instead, he found himself saying, "Just a trim, if you please." Aden's hair was so beautiful, with its riot of color and silky strands. He found he couldn't bear to have it disturbed.

Mr. Haddad nodded and gestured toward the chair.

James walked Aden over and reluctantly let go of his hand to stand away and give the barber the space he needed.

Mr. Haddad hummed as he scrutinized Aden's head, sifting through it with his fingers. Finally, he picked up his scissors and got to work. In no time, he was done, Aden looking pretty much as he had when he came in, only neater. Haddad had somehow managed to make the strands of hair fall into a more tamed manner without losing much of its length.

Haddad brushed Aden's neck and shoulders, then stood back. "There. Is good, yes?"

James nodded. "Yes. Perfect as always, Mr. Haddad. Thank you."

James pulled out sufficient coin from his pocket, paid the barber, and tugged Aden by his hand out of the chair. The familiar was touching his hair with his free hand, saying nothing, yet looking happy.

"Do you like it?"

Aden nodded. "It's nice. The woman who cut hair at the Academy wasn't nearly so skilled."

James harumphed. "I should expect not. Mr. Haddad comes from a long line of barbers. Since he set up his shop here, I've never gone anywhere else. Are you hungry?" He didn't bother to wait for an answer. He, himself, was starved. "We'll pick something up for dinner from the deli. It's a special day and we deserve a treat."

James couldn't help smiling as he led the way to buy some chicken and dumpling soup from the nearby restaurant and then return to the apartment. He pulled two bowls and spoons from the shelves and the drawer and handed them to Aden.

"Set the table, please. The soup is still warm so I won't bother to heat it more."

He carried the container to the table and ladled some into each bowl while Aden fetched napkins, glasses and the pitcher of water without being told. The hominess of it made James ridiculously happy. He'd expected an awkwardness as they got to know each other, but so far they were settling into their new life fairly easily. At least he was.

He waited until they'd both had a few spoonsful of soup before checking with Aden.

"How are you feeling about today? I mean, it's a big change for you." He was surprised to find himself tensing as he waited for a response.

The familiar stared at him with wide eyes for a few seconds before answering. "It's been lovely, thank you. I appreciate your generosity." He quickly lowered his gaze as he spooned up more soup.

James frowned. "I'm glad you're...okay with your new situation, but I don't want you to think this relationship is all about my willingness to spend money on you." He swallowed more food as he contemplated what to say next. "I mean, this business is for both of us. We're going to be working as a team, each important in his own way. And, you know, you'll have an allowance for your part of the work to spend how you want."

He hadn't really worked out the numbers, but he didn't want to be like his father, controlling the purse strings so much that James' mother had to practically beg for what she needed.

Aden didn't reply right away, simply continued to eat and drink. Then, "Thank you, but I prefer you keep all the money. I wouldn't know what to spend it on and shopkeepers don't have to serve familiars anyway."

James frowned again, deeper this time. "They do if your witch is with you." *Stupid laws.* Familiars were treated as if they didn't have the brains or self-control to manage their own finances. Again much like the way women were treated by both the law and their husbands. It made his blood boil.

Aden shrugged as he scraped the bottom of his bowl. "If you have to be with me, you may as well hold the money, too."

James couldn't argue with that logic. "Well, we'll figure it out."

After supper, Aden cleaned the dishes without being asked, which James appreciated. He'd been warned that familiars, especially cat-based ones, could be lazy. Obviously, that was incorrect, or perhaps Aden was a cut above his species. No matter. James sat by an open window, enjoying the night breeze, and read by the lamp he'd turned on as the sun set.

When he was done, Aden came and knelt beside James' chair. It took him a moment to registerer the fact. Reading absorbed his attention, something his father and brother never understood. They preferred more manly pursuits like cards or checkers. It was yet one more way that James was different from the rest of his family. His mother had always warned him he'd strain his eyes with all his reading, and while he somewhat missed the warm glow of gas lighting, electricity made it easier to see the words on the page. He wasn't worried about needing glasses yet.

He closed the book and glanced around the room. He hadn't considered before that he had only one chair to relax in. Another one would have to be procured for Aden. He pictured the two of them sitting on either side of the hearth, reading in the quiet of the night after a good day's work. The simple domesticity of it warmed him in a way he hadn't expected.

James stood and held out his hand. "Come on. I don't expect you to kneel on the floor, for good Christ's sake. Let's get ready for bed and we can relax there before going to sleep."

Chapter Three

Aden didn't hesitate to take James' hand and stand, but there was a sudden wariness in his eyes. And he kept his gaze on the floor. His slender neck rippled with a hard swallow. It took James a few seconds to pinpoint the boy's apprehension.

"I'm not going to mount you again tonight." As much as he wanted to, he wasn't such a cad that he'd forgotten how sore the boy must be.

Aden blinked rapidly but didn't look at him. "As you say. I understand that my body belongs to you and you can do whatever you want with it."

Fury rose within him. "Bullshit!" He lowered his temper at Aden's blink. "I mean, that's not true. I'm your witch, not your slave master. We fought a bloody great war to get rid of that obscenity. It makes no sense to continue to apply it to familiars. Your comfort is just as important as my rights as your witch. We'll make these decisions together."

Aden looked skeptical. "Yes, sir. James," he quickly corrected.

"Good. Now come on, let's get ready for bed."

It turned out that familiars took very little care. Aden could clean every part of himself simply by shifting to animal form, then back again. The bath he'd drawn the boy earlier hadn't strictly been necessary, yet he hoped it had been a soothing experience. It was James who required a bath to wash off the grime of the day and he briefly considered how fun it might be to take one together. Instead, he sent Aden off to bed while he bathed alone, then joined him once he'd dried off and washed his teeth and mouth. He was pleased to see the boy lying naked in human form, although he shot James another wary look as he joined him.

The reaction was no surprise, given that the sight of the beautiful familiar laid out for the taking had made James instantly and achingly hard. He couldn't hide his arousal as he whipped off the towel and got onto the bed.

He waved his hand at his erection. "This has a mind of its own but my promise still stands. No mounting. However, there are things we can do to please us both. I want you to enjoy being with me, Aden. It's more fun for me too if you do."

"Okay." Aden's response made it clear he wasn't convinced.

Well, James would just have to show him. He lay on his side, facing the boy. "Turn towards me."

Aden didn't hesitate, his bright green eyes staring at him with more curiosity than fear.

James slid close so that his cock brushed against the familiar's stomach. He hissed at the sensation and fought back the need to press against the boy's body and rub himself to completion. What he was about to do was totally unfamiliar but he knew enough to make his efforts successful. He reached out tentatively to clasp Aden's limp cock. The familiar startled at the touch.

"It's okay. I'm going to do my best to make this good for both of us. Do you trust me?" He held his breath until the boy nodded. "Good."

Firming his grip, he jerked the familiar's shaft much as he'd do to himself. The angle was different but everything else worked the same way. It didn't take long for the cock to swell within his grip and become fully erect.

"That's a good boy. Feels nice, huh?"

Aden nodded as he gnawed his lower lip and balled his hands into fists.

"Close your eyes, baby. This is going to get better."

When Aden complied, James opened his hand to clasp both their cocks. He couldn't quite close the circle around both shafts and it took a while for him to find his rhythm. Soon, though, he was jerking the dicks together with the same vigor he would use when desperate to find a release to get to sleep. This time, his urgency was born of an almost unbridled need to come.

The familiar scrunched up his eyes and his breath huffed out as his slender chest rose and fell rapidly. The obvious pleasure the boy was getting spurred James to speed up his efforts. His balls tightened in a clear sign he was about to come. He wanted to hold back until he was sure Aden was ready but lacked the control. He shouted out his release, his cock bucking in his grasp, throwing off his rhythm. It didn't matter because, joy of joy, Aden was coming too. Warm cum splashed over James' fingers, slicking the way for him to jerk them both until they were dry.

Spent more than usual, it took James a while to regain his sense. When he did, he smiled.

Aden was fast asleep.

* * * *

Aden stood looking up at the sign. It was hard to focus on anything other than the strange feelings he'd had since waking up next to James. Although he'd had little of it in his life, he was pretty sure the feeling was one of guarded happiness. His body still tingled from what James had done to him the previous night. It had been and continued to be amazing. Some of the boys at the Academy had helped each other out like that occasionally. It didn't mean anything except finding a bit of relief from the grinding misery of their lives.

This was different. It wasn't merely the ecstasy of the pleasure. He felt closer to James emotionally and couldn't wait for it to happen again. Hopefully it would. He was under no illusions that his witch would be satisfied with that kind of thing. James would want to mount him again, probably most every day. At least that was what he'd been told. The bond needed reinforcement routinely. If he were lucky, though, James might afford him the pleasure of having the man's hand bring him to completion, too. If that were the case, he figured he could get used to the other.

"What do you think?"

Aden cocked his head and stared at the sign some more. *Raven Detective Agency, Seeker Witch.* A picture of the dark bird taking flight was etched next to the lettering.

"Why Raven?"

"It's my last name. Byrne translates loosely to raven. I thought it would be catchy because, you know, I find people and things, like a bird taking wing."

Aden turned to his witch. "Why didn't you get a bird familiar?"

James flashed a smile. "I thought of it but they are tough to come by and I also wanted a familiar who could slink into hard-to-get places and be helpful in a fight. Not that I expect there to be much of any violence," he added, cupping Aden's chin. "I won't let anything bad happen to you. I promise."

Aden wasn't sure the witch could keep it, but he was too happy to worry about it. He smiled instead. A warm tingle shot through him when James took his hand and led him into the building. The office was on the second floor and had a reception area with a few chairs and a desk that fed into the office. It wasn't big but it was well-furnished with a large wooden desk, a Persian rug and two sturdy wing-backed leather chairs for clients. As with the apartment, it had electric lights, proving once again that his witch was a man of some means.

"I want to spruce this up a bit when I have the money and hope to have enough business soon to hire someone to man the reception desk." James led him over to a bay window with an upholstered seat. "I figure this is where you can spend your days. Clients will be impressed seeing you, and it gets good sun in the afternoon. Go ahead and give it a try."

Aden quickly disrobed and, putting his smock and slippers neatly aside, he shifted and jumped onto the window seat, already warm from the morning sunlight. He stretched out and started to purr. He couldn't help it. He was that happy.

James peered down at him and smiled. "You're adorable and just a little fierce. I'll leave you to nap."

Aden wanted to say he didn't need to sleep, but being in his snow leopard form and with a full belly, he couldn't help closing his eyes and doing just that.

* * * *

Aden woke abruptly to the sound of voices—one was James and the other was…female. He pricked up his ears without opening his eyes, curious but not wanting to draw attention to himself.

"Please have a seat, Mrs. Appleton."

"Thank you, Mr. Byrne." The woman had the kind of Brahim accent the Boston elite who patronized the Academy used whenever they visited to peruse the children as if they were specimens in a museum.

There was the scraping of a chair and Aden dared to open his eyes to slits. James sat behind his deck, smiling at the woman seated in one of the visitor chairs. The woman was indeed dressed in finery that spoke of great wealth. Aden couldn't help wondering why this woman would come to James for anything. While James had a bit more coin than most and the office was in a respectable business neighborhood, the rich had their own sources for everything. And didn't people come to them?

What is this woman doing here?

The supposed client held her hand to the front of her throat where she wore some kind of jewelry.

"I imagine you've heard of my husband. He's a prominent financier in town."

James nodded. "Of course, madam. His reputation is well-known. I, um…does he know you're here?"

Mrs. Appleton lowered her gaze demurely. "Not exactly." She leaned forward. "You see, he is quite ill."

"Oh, I'm very sorry to hear that."

"Yes, well, he doesn't have long I'm afraid." Before saying more, the woman pulled a handkerchief from her reticule and dabbed at the corners of what appeared to be very dry eyes. "I've come out of love. I'm desperately trying to find our son."

James sat up straighter. "You have a missing child? Have you informed the police?"

"No." Mrs. Appleton once more lowered her gaze. "He's an adult, you see. I say 'our son', but the truth is he's from my husband's first marriage. I tried to be more of an older sister to him given that we aren't that far apart in age." Her cheeks bloomed with a faint pink.

"I see." James gave a tight smile. "I take it he left under somewhat strained circumstances?"

"Yes." Mrs. Appleton dabbed those dry eyes some more. "This is very hard to say but Josiah, our son, has a…fondness for other men. You understand?"

James nodded gravely.

"His father could never accept that, as you can well imagine. There were words exchanged, harsh ones, and Josiah moved out. My husband, as he nears his end, regrets that falling out and wants very much to reconcile with Josiah before it's too late."

"Of course, I understand. Very commendable of him." James pulled a sheet of paper in front of him and dipped his pen in the inkwell. "What can you tell me about him that might help me find him?"

Mrs. Appleton cleared her throat. "I can tell you that he's somewhere in, ah, Freaktown."

James winced, a brief expression that Mrs. Appleton couldn't help seeing.

"You understand now why I need your help. I've approached friends on the police force but they rarely go into that part of town, as you may know."

"Yes, I do. It's a tough neighborhood and as no respectable people live there, the police mostly choose to ignore what happens within it."

Aden bit back a hiss. Even at the Academy he'd heard of Freaktown. It was where unbonded familiars and other undesirables, like homosexuals, went to live their lives unmolested by all of those 'respectable people'. He'd been warned plenty of times that it was where his future lay if he didn't bond properly with a witch.

"Exactly, Mr. Byrne. And, no offense meant, but seeker witches that cater to higher society won't go there, either. I'm hoping that you are more... adventurous."

Desperate for work was what the woman really meant. Aden was affronted on James' behalf.

But if the witch felt any insult, he didn't betray it. "As a former police officer, I have some limited experience with the area. Do you have something of Josiah's that I can tap into?"

"Yes." She reached once more into her reticule. "I understood you'd need an object belonging to him. Will this do?" She held out a tortoiseshell comb.

James took it, held it tightly in his hand and closed his eyes. He took a deep breath, then let it out while opening his eyes. "Yes. This will do nicely, especially as I have a familiar to boost my power."

Now the woman looked in Aden's direction. She stiffened. "I don't like cats as a rule, but as it helps you, I of course have no objection. So long as I don't have to interact with the creature," she added.

Aden took no offense because he wanted nothing to do with her, either. Fortunately, he didn't have to. That was James' worry. He closed his eyes, letting the drone of the voices wash over him. There was some further discussion about fees and such. Soon the sound of retreating steps and a door closing met his ears. He opened his eyes again when he heard James approach.

The man was grinning ear-to-ear and rubbing his hands. "You caught all of that?"

Aden shifted and sat up. "Yes. I don't like her." He couldn't help making his feelings known, not that they counted one whit.

"Neither do I. But she paid half my fee up front and, given that I quoted double my usual amount the moment I clapped eyes on her, I've really been paid in full already. If…no, when we find her stepson, word will reach others of her class and that may mean more work. One can hope, anyway." James returned to his desk and dropped into his chair. "Up until now, I've spent my power finding lost pets and the occasional frippery that people misplace." He picked up the comb. "With our bond, I feel so much more." He barked out a laugh. "It's exhilarating, more than I ever dreamed." He smiled at Aden. "It's all thanks to you."

Rather embarrassed at the naked appreciation, Aden looked away. "Are we going to, um, Freaktown now?"

James shook his head. "No. I need time to sit and focus on his whereabouts so that I can track him more precisely. We'll get something to eat first, then return home. I can be more comfortable there, lying on my bed."

A little tingle tickled Aden's insides down low. He wondered if James would need a bonding boost by mounting him. The thought should have frightened him yet somehow didn't.

* * * *

"Are you feeling all right?" James had to shout the question above the roar of his motor car. Despite not wanting to impose on his familiar too much, he'd realized a boost in the bonding would give him his best chance for success this night. He'd been careful with Aden and had jerked him off afterward, but he could tell he was still hurting the boy. Guilt was nudging out his excitement over his first real case.

"I'm fine." Aden's soft voice barely carried.

James wasn't sure whether it was because the boy was normally soft-spoken or because he was hurting too much to give a convincing answer.

Can't be helped. Damn it.

James forced himself to put aside his worry and focus on his job. He parked just outside the invisible line between Freaktown and the rest of Boston. As a witch, he'd never felt the repugnance of his fellow coppers entering into the neighborhood. He understood their feelings, however. No one was typical in this part of town and, like any neighborhood filled with desperate people, it had its dangers. He patted his pocket where he'd placed his revolver just in case they ran into trouble that fists couldn't handle. He was determined, too, not to force Aden into any fight on his behalf.

He put the crank shaft into the satchel he'd brought for Aden's things and shot his familiar what he hoped was a reassuring smile. "Let's go."

He'd spent the afternoon holding onto Josiah Appleton's comb and picturing in his mind's eye the man's location and the best route to get to him. The images were lodged securely in his inner vision, so he didn't expect to need to touch the comb again. Nevertheless, he'd packed that, too. Just in case. There was something very strange about being hired by the second Mrs. Appleton. When a beautiful young woman married a much older, rich man, it was due to either family pressure to form an economic alliance or her own desire for wealth and standing. Although he had no personal experience, his impression was that stepchildren didn't always get along with their stepmother. It seemed odd to him that this woman would go out of her way to mend fences between her husband and his son. Didn't the estrangement benefit her financially?

Perhaps, or maybe he was being too hard on the woman's character on such short acquaintance. In any event, he couldn't put his finger on what might be going on. All he knew for sure was that a wealthy woman had hired him and paid his fee, which he'd raised on the spot without a single qualm. He couldn't afford to turn her down. Besides, the Brahmins lived their lives differently from other people. Who was he to worry about what they did with and to each other?

A heavy atmosphere hung over Freaktown, more so than other impoverished neighborhoods. Most of Boston was made up of areas packed with people who shared a cultural or religious background. His own family still lived in Southie, a place known for its Irish population. Those were ties that bound the inhabitants together and gave it a certain...flavor that spoke of their heritage. The people living in Freaktown were more diverse, tied only by the shared situation of being outcasts, although he supposed there might be various blocks that were populated by similar beings. He'd never thought much of it, but likely the unbonded familiars stuck together and the homosexual men likewise supported each other. It was a matter of survival after all, and there was nothing to keep any of the people in Freaktown from preying on each other. The police hardly ever came into this part of town, as he and Mrs. Appleton had discussed, and then only to protect the public outside of these environs.

As they proceeded farther into the area, people eyed them with suspicion. More than one familiar darted off, almost certainly afraid that he was a witch looking to force bonding on them. It was a despicable thing to do, yet some witches had no sense of honor or decency and would rather steal a familiar than pay for one. James grabbed Aden's hand to keep him close. It was entirely possible rogue witches wandered these streets, too, and he wasn't taking any chances with his boy.

It wasn't all misery he saw. There were shops, closed for the day, but which spoke of commerce. Laundry hung from lines strung along balconies of apartments. Some of the sidewalks had been swept clean, while a block over here or there was nothing but muddy ruts. He allowed himself to goggle at the sights and could tell Aden was doing the same. At this point, his witch sense kept him on the right path to Josiah. The closer he got, the stronger the tug, as if a string pulled him toward the young man. Not surprisingly, when they turned a corner toward the harborside, there were greater signs of life. The night was underway and lots of taverns and bawdy houses were open for business. Catcalls tried to lure him toward various vices, but he headed straight for the only place that mattered.

Bottoms Up was typical for its type of drinking establishment. There was a tough watching the door and looked ready to deny them entrance until James pulled out a magic coin that disappeared into the man's pocket within a blink of an eye. The interior was dim and about half-full of men who hooted and clapped at the singer on stage. At least those who were watching egged on the rude song that accompanied a slow striptease. Dark corners held couples entwined in each other's embrace, seemingly unconcerned about the public nature of their displays. James figured most of the couples were fancy boys working for the tavern who would try their best to entice clients up the staircase near the bar.

All of this was peripheral to James' view. His attention was taken by the piano player bathed in a soft glow that transcended that of the gaslights. It was one of the more intriguing parts of his witch gift that his quarry shone like a lighthouse beacon to his eyes. There was no question that Josiah Appleton sat on the stool, his fingers pounding away on the keys. The man looked to be having a merry time playing for the stripping singer.

He had succeeded. Now all he needed to do was to persuade young Appleton to return to the family fold.

Chapter Four

James couldn't hold back a grin as he leaned to speak into Aden's ear. "That's him at the piano."

Aden whipped his head back to James, having been staring around the dark, smokey tavern with wide eyes. "These are all men."

James chuckled. "Of course they are, baby. Mr. Appleton is a homosexual. This tavern caters to them. Some of these patrons are from more respectable parts of town. They come here because they know they can find what they want without anyone judging them or turning them over to the police. We'll have to wait until there is a break in the entertainment to speak with Appleton."

He led Aden over to the bar on the far end and leaned against it to get the bartender's attention. The young man with a stunningly beautiful face, powdered and rouged, sauntered over to them.

"What will it be, handsome?" The boy batted his eyelashes.

"Two sarsaparillas, please." Even if he weren't on the job, he would never dare consume whatever rot gut they served here. The alcohol was probably distilled in the basement.

The bartender pouted. "Playing it safe. I admire that in a man, but if you decide to get more adventurous, my break is in thirty minutes."

James tugged Aden closer and put his arm around him. "Thank you, a most generous offer, but, as you can see, I'm all set in that area."

He didn't bother to add that what he shared with Aden was different. James had no interest in bedding another man. Only his familiar elicited that desire in him, and damn if the mere thought of it made his trousers snug.

The bartender shrugged, then went to get their drinks. When he slapped the bottles on the counter, James pulled out more than enough to pay for them.

He held up the coin. "When the piano player has a break, please tell him I'd love to speak with him."

The bartender narrowed his gaze, then shrugged again and took the coin. "Sure thing, handsome."

James took the drinks and led Aden over to a table by a wall. From there, he could see both Appleton and the front door. It never hurt to keep alert and guard one's back. His vigilance didn't stop him from noticing the flash of delight when Aden took a sip from his bottle.

"Have you never had sarsaparilla before?"

The familiar shook his head. "No. We didn't have much money when I was little for treats and the Academy didn't believe in spoiling us."

James' heart ached for the boy. Even his father had made sure to find money for the occasional treat for his kids, and he wasn't an indulgent man as a rule. James vowed that he could rectify the situation himself. He would shower Aden with little pleasures whenever he could.

Loud clapping and whistles brought his attention back to the stage. The performer was now completely naked. The boy shook his privates, which were tied in a red ribbon bow, then turned to expose his backside to the leering men. He blew kisses as he left the stage and about a dozen men got up to crowd around the performer, no doubt putting in their bids to take him to bed.

James' attention didn't linger on the display for long. He tracked Appleton's movements as the man left his stool and headed to the bar. The bartender pointed James out even as he handed the man a drink of clear liquid in a shot glass. Appleton's gaze narrowed before he tossed the liquor back, then sauntered over. He stood in front of James with one hand on his hip and a suspicious look on his face. He was dressed in masculine clothing, albeit with bold colors and ruffles at the neck and cuffs. His brown hair was pulled back into a stubby tail.

"What does a witch and his familiar want with me? I don't fuck for money, only play the piano...for your information."

Before James could reassure the young man that he had no carnal intentions, the bartender returned with another glass of alcohol, this time dark in color and filling a cut glass nearly to the brim, and put it on the table in front of Appleton. Appleton plopped onto the empty seat and gestured toward the drink.

"I do, however, expect patrons to pay for my libations."

James plucked another coin out of his pocket and handed it over to the bartender without a glance. He didn't need his witch's sense to pick this man out as definitely different from anyone else working in the establishment. The man sitting opposite him was cultured and educated, not the typical kind of man one found living in Freaktown. Josiah must have had no money to access after his break with his father. It would have had to have been a hellish fight with his father for the young man to sink so low as this. At least he wasn't selling his body — yet. The performer was undoubtedly making far more that night than his accompanist.

The connection having been made, the bright aura around Appleton disappeared. The tie between them loosened too. With his quarry found, it was now a matter of human effort to convince the boy to return home. James had already decided on the blunt approach.

"I'm here to convince you to go home to see your father, Josiah. If I may call you that."

The boy took a sip of his whiskey before replying. Nothing in his expression betrayed his feelings. "I prefer to be called Josie. And you are either a liar or insane. My father would never send someone to fetch me back. We despise each other."

"I'm afraid circumstances have changed." James licked his lower lip. "Your father is…dying. I'm so sorry."

Josie raised his eyebrows. "It's about time. The devil has certainly taken his time calling in his marker."

"I understand there are hard feelings between you, but your stepmother says his dying wish is to reconcile with you."

"*Melinda*?" Josie's tone was the kind one might use when saying dog shit after finding it stuck to the bottom of his shoe. "Did she hire you? Because let me assure you that viper wouldn't bother to present me to my father even if he did want to kiss and make up. Which he does not. Believe me, I've known the man my entire life. He bends for no one and under no condition would he change his mind about what he thinks of the disgusting acts I get up to."

Josie drained his glass and signaled for another.

James frowned and glanced at Aden, who looked at him and shrugged.

"Surely, this is a unique situation. He's never been dying before." James heard the strain in his own voice and wondered who he was trying to convince, Josie or himself?

Instead of replying, Josie turned his attention to Aden, while waiting for his drink to be refilled. "Did you bond of your own free will? Because if you didn't, you can stay here. There are places in Freaktown that help familiars break free."

James wanted to jump in and demand Josie mind his own business but, as James was intruding on the man's family matters, it would be rather hypocritical of him. Besides, Aden's opinion about his fate wasn't irrelevant. It was a legitimate question, even if it were a rude one. And James wasn't worried about Aden's answer. Surely the boy was happy with his situation? James was being good to him, unless one counted his clumsy bedding of the boy. That wasn't intentional cruelty. He just needed time to find a better way to go about it, that was all.

Aden glanced his way before answering. "I was sold to James by the Academy my parents put me in. No one asked me what I wanted, but I like being bonded to James. He's been kind to me and his work is interesting." He glanced at his surroundings. "I wouldn't want to live here. No offense."

Josie sat back in his chair. "Oh, sweetie, no one *wants* to live in Freaktown. But only you can decide whether you like your current life or not. I hated mine and anything here is better than being in that mausoleum of a home, kowtowing to my hideous father and his greedy bitch of a wife. Besides, everything they have is ill-gotten gain."

Dread settled into James' belly. He'd ignored his suspicions of Mrs. Appleton in favor of his first case. Now, he had to scrutinize what he'd gotten involved with.

"What do you mean by that?"

Josie sipped his drink and gave James what could be described as a pitying look. "Where do you think my father's wealth comes from?"

James furrowed his brow. "You're Appletons. Boston Brahmins. Wealth is part of your heritage."

Josie twirled his glass on the table. "Oh sure. Generations ago, we Appletons managed to make a packet of money, but with each generation, that pile dwindles unless someone adds to it. And if you're not the first-born son, your share is considerably lower. My direct ancestors were born in the wrong order. By the time my father reached his majority, the pickings were slim indeed.

"His intellect is far too dim for him to become an academic and he certainly wasn't fit to enter the clergy. And of course entering a trade was out of the question, even if he could master some valuable skill. Which he could not." Josie folded his arms on the table and leaned in to stare at James. "He'd thought he'd married well but that money dried up soon enough. If I had a maternal legacy to fall back on, do you think I'd be putting my boring piano lessons to work here?"

The knot tightened. "Your stepmother was dripping in expensive jewelry and wearing the height of fashion. He made money somehow."

"Oh yes…from blackmail."

James couldn't stop his mouth from dropping open.

"Delicious, isn't it? The great Robert Appleton, member of the best clubs, invitee to the best parties, was clever enough to keep his eyes and ears open. Every dirty secret he learned turned into buckets of money. He has something on just about everyone in this town and in the state, for that matter. Hell," he added, sitting back once more, "the country."

James huffed out a breath and wiped his brow. It was getting hot in the tavern as it filled with more patrons and he was beginning to fear he'd been thrown into the worst kind of shit. No, not thrown. He'd jumped feet first with enthusiasm.

"How does this play into your stepmother asking me to find you?"

"Hmm. There's an interesting question, sweetie. I can only speculate, but I can tell you that I inherited my father's nose for dirt. I found out where he kept his book."

"What book?"

"*The* book. A ledger not unlike what I assume the devil keeps on people's lives. Every detail of his victims—identity, scandal, amounts paid, amounts owed. There are a lot of powerful people who'd love to get their hands on it either to destroy the information on themselves or to pick up where my father is leaving off." He raised his hands. "Perhaps Melinda is trying to cash in on it, too. For all her skills in bed to keep dear papa happy, he never told her where the book was."

"Was?"

Josie gave him a look of pure glee. "I stole it."

James rubbed his chin as he considered the implications of what he was hearing. "Did you blackmail him over it, get a pile of money to hand it back? Of course not. You wouldn't be here if you did. There are plenty of places in Europe where you could live your life freely and well."

"You're exactly right about that. I could be rolling in silk sheets with some adorable Greek boy, but I have standards. A moral compass that came from God knows where. Although to be fair, I did warn my father not to interfere with my life or I'd hand it over to *The Boston Globe*. As long as he left me alone, I promised to keep it secret." He lowered his gaze and his expression turned somber. "I just wanted to be left alone."

Things clicked into place. "Melinda knows that you have it and wants to get it for herself, not your father."

"Aren't you the clever one, sweetie. It's the only reason she'd send someone to find me. As much as he's made from his little hobby, they're extravagant in their spending. There's probably no big nest egg for her once the old man kicks it. If she has the book, she can pick up where he left off, only she won't have to share it with anyone. I won't give it to her."

"No. I wouldn't want you to."

It was James' own sense of right and wrong that had gotten him kicked off the force. He hadn't taken a stand then simply to give in to the dark temptation of using his power to make a fast and large amount of money. But what to do now? His client expected results and if he confronted her about what he'd learned, what would she do in retaliation? His business might go under through her influence before it got off the ground.

His decision-making was interrupted by a loud, shrill whistle and a shriek of "Raid". Then all hell broke loose as coppers poured in the front door, Billy clubs raised. There was a shock of inaction for about a second before patrons reacted in blind panic, trying to push past the raiders while avoiding being clouted. James had been stunned in disbelief as much as anyone, but came to his senses just as quickly. He grabbed both Aden and Josie by the arms and dragged them toward the door behind the bar. His training had caused him to scope out an escape route from the moment he'd entered the tavern. He was glad he'd done so now.

They entered a storeroom moments after the bartender had made his escape, except that the poor boy squealed in outrage as a couple of coppers caught him just outside it. Of course the police had covered every exit. But James had something mere humans did not. He backed into the corner of the room, hugging Aden and Josie close to his sides.

"Don't make a sound," he whispered before focusing on his cloaking power. As good as he was at finding things, he could also hide himself and others to whom he extended the shield. It was a drain on his strength and he couldn't hold it for long. Then again, he didn't have to. One cop dragged the bartender back into the main room while shouting to the other to guard the inner door. When the second copper's back was turned, James edged toward then out of the open exit. The fetid smell of the alley nearly took his attention away from his cloaking. He hurried away from the building before his power gave out.

He pressed Aden and Josie against the side of the building next door. "Stay here and keep quiet. I'm going to see if there's a safe route out of here."

He slipped away and crept down the alley.

Aden struggled to slow his breaths. His heart felt as if it would burst from fear. The shock of the raid was something he couldn't shake off, however. Up until that point, it had seemed like a quiet conversation that had confirmed his instincts about Mrs. Appleton. It all sounded very sordid and he had no idea what James was going to do next, but that was okay. It wasn't his job to figure out stuff like that. James would. The man's quick action had saved them from being carted off in a paddy wagon, although he wasn't sure what he and James had done wrong. And what were the police doing there anyway? Hadn't the whole point of hiring James been based on the coppers giving Freaktown a wide berth?

He wasn't sure what James' power had done back in the storeroom. Familiars weren't given a lot of information about their witch's power. Whatever it had been, it had gotten them this far, but if James had been able to sustain it, he wouldn't be waiting here for the man to return. What if there were no escape routes possible, and what would the police do to James if he were caught trying to flee?

"I'm fine. Stop worrying about me."

Aden startled at the voice inside his head before relaxing. Of course, the bond. They could communicate telepathically over short distances. Knowing that James was nearby and connected to him helped ease his worries.

Then suddenly James was back. He leaned to speak lowly in Aden's ear. "The end of the alley is blocked with cops and I can't see which way to go to avoid them. I need you to shift and get on the roof. Find us a way out from that vantage point. Can you do that?"

Aden nodded once, happy to have a role to play at last. He stripped off his smock and shifted out of his slippers. Using crates, he bounded up to the roof of the building to look around. The air was fresher than it had been in the alley, although the entire area of the city was shrouded in a kind of smokey despair. At least that was how he felt as he slunk over to the edge of the roof for a look around.

"It's okay, baby. You're doing great."

James' encouragement helped him shake off the gloomy feeling and concentrate on his job. Shouts and shrieks shot up from the street and his nose quivered at the smell of blood. The cops weren't being gentle as they herded their prisoners into paddy wagons. The horses pulling them snorted and stamped in agitation. Aden didn't have to look down to know that way was dangerous. So he bounded back to the edge of the roof above the alley and leapt over to the building next door. The sounds of the raid diminished in this direction, although the front of the building was the scene of a certain amount of action. Coppers patrolled back and forth, slapping their batons in their palms, clearly itching for a fight. Other than the beleaguered patrons of the tavern, no one else stirred in the area. The residents of Freaktown obviously knew when to lie low.

The opposite end of the roof was different, however. Although a copper leaned against the back of the tavern, smoking as he watched for anyone escaping the raid, his view didn't extend to the alley past the next-door building. Enough refuse piled along the walls, as well as the rough brick of which they were built, could give James and Josie the means to climb up, then down. If they were quiet and fast, they might evade notice. If not, there was cover on the roof for them to wait out the raid. Aden hurried back to let James know. Of course, the witch already had the knowledge, given his tie to Aden's thoughts. By the time he'd returned to the two men, James was already leading Josie up to the roof where Aden waited. Aden shifted as they joined him, flattened to avoid being seen.

"I'm going to see if I can hear anything of use," James whispered. "Stay here." He took a moment to ruffle Aden's hair and shoot him a grin before crawling away.

Josie's face was ashen as he lay with it cradled in his hands. The poor man looked both furious and as if he were holding back tears. Aden put what he hoped was a comforting hand on the man's arm, too scared to try to give him words of comfort for fear of making noise.

James bellied back up to them. "They're looking for you, Josie. I heard the detective in charge dressing the sergeant down for not finding you already. They're not going to leave any time soon, so we may as well take advantage of the chaos out front while we can."

The witch started crawling to the far end of the opposite side. Aden followed with Josie by his side. When he reached the edge, Aden shifted again and bounded down to keep watch. He gave James a silent confirmation that the coast was as clear as it could be. The two men started the difficult journey of climbing down. It was no surprise that James was both strong and agile. Josie did valiantly well, but at the last point, he tipped some boxes over as he stepped to the ground. James pushed Josie against the wall and they disappeared right before Aden's eyes. Except he could sense they were still there because James was inside him too, now.

Footsteps had Aden peering around the corner. The cop guarding the back of the tavern was coming toward them, baton at the ready. Knowing James didn't have unlimited power to stay invisible, he struggled to come up with a way to distract the cop. If he simply leapt out at the man, he'd be announcing their presence for sure. Unlike a dog familiar, or something else that was pet-like, a leopard of any kind was going to be recognized as a familiar.

Salvation and inspiration came in the form of an alley cat. The poor creature crept out from behind a pile of rubbish, hissing at Aden. He didn't hesitate to chase it out of the alley. It ran straight at the copper, hissing and screeching before racing away. The man stopped, shook his head, then turned back to his post. Aden panted with relief and sat waiting for James to come to him. When the witch did, with Josie in tow, the three of them slid away from the alley and walked quietly in the opposite direction from which he and James had entered.

They didn't stop until the noise of the raid couldn't be heard anymore. It was James, of course, who decided they could stop and rest. He pulled into yet another alley, this one closer to the harbor, and leaned against a brick wall.

"Holy Mary, mother of God."

Josie slumped next to him. "I told you Melinda was a cold-heartened snake. In the nearly one year since I've been working at the tavern, there's never been a raid. Cops don't bother coming into Freaktown."

Aden shifted to human form and stood, awkwardly naked, beside his witch. He wasn't sure whether he should stay as a leopard and waited for James to perhaps chastise him. Instead, the man opened his pack and wordlessly handed him his smock and slippers. Aden gratefully put them on. It felt natural to be only in his skin when he was with James. Being so in front of another person was a different matter.

James shook his head as he spoke to Josie. "I don't get it. You think Melinda used me to find you, then had the cops…what, follow me and raid the place to get you?"

Josie's expression answered the question so clearly Aden had no trouble reading it.

"That's crazy!" James clamped his lips shut and looked around to see if his outburst had caught attention.

Nothing stirred, although Aden sensed there were eyes on them.

"That's crazy," James repeated in a low voice. "Why would she come to me? I'm hardly the only seeker witch in the city."

"She'd never risk using one who caters to our class for a couple of reasons. One is that I'm an embarrassment to her and my father. I'm sure they've told everyone I'm off visiting the continent, or some such nonsense. Second, she'd fear word of the book getting out. I'm sure she assumed you'd see only her coin and not ask any questions, and if you're picked up in a raid on a homosexual bawdy house?" He shrugged. "Who would care? You'd be too humiliated to say anything to anyone. And if you made any noise, she'd simply pay you more."

James slapped his palm against his forehead. "The perfect patsy."

Emotions emanating from his witch swamped Aden. The intensity and mix of them alarmed him. He tried to put a comforting hand on James' arm, but found himself in a quick, hard hug instead.

"It'll be fine, baby. Don't worry." To Josie he said, "We need to hide you somewhere safe until I figure out what to do. I know the perfect place. Let's get back to where I left my automobile and I'll take you there."

When Josie didn't move to follow, James clamped a hand on the man's shoulder. "Melinda was wrong about me. I do care, and I can't be bought off. Using me has made me mad and if she'd done any research into me at all, she'd know I don't just get mad. I get even."

Chapter Five

Aden would have far preferred sitting on James' lap and clinging to him as they whisked through the dark, quiet streets of Boston. But as the witch had to operate the vehicle, Aden was stuck being perched on Josie, with his eyes closed against the rushing wind in his face. The young Mr. Appleton was surprisingly quiet and even sanguine about the frightening few hours they had just spent. He seemed resigned, as if he'd expected no less than to be hunted by his father and stepmother. It made Aden wonder what horrors existed for rich families behind the drawn drapes of their stately homes. He hadn't known much in the way of kindness in his childhood but at least his parents hadn't actively worked to make his life miserable. That had simply been a byproduct of their own fear. Whatever money they'd received from his sale to James, Aden was sure it was incidental to their primary motive of removing from their home something they didn't understand or want.

James took them down rutted streets as the town homes of the wealthy gave way to tenements. This part of the city would soon come alive as the residents were used to rising early to start their day in a manner that served the more affluent. So when James finally turned into an alley and stopped the automobile, Aden blew a sigh of relief that their journey was soon to end. Looking around, he was surprised to see they were in the mews of a large, stone church. He didn't have much time to ponder the oddity of their destination because James was suddenly standing at the passenger side of the vehicle, lifting Aden off Josie's lap. Aden allowed himself to be distracted by the wonderful sensation of being cradled in his witch's arms. The experience was over too quickly. James set him on his feet and went to ring the bell of the nearby dark house.

Aden would never have questioned what James was doing. Josie had no such reluctance. He joined James on the stoop with hands on his hips.

"What are we doing at a church? My kind aren't welcome, as I'm sure you're aware, and this isn't even my religion."

James spared the man a glance while ringing the bell again. "This is the rectory, not the church. And it's the safest place I know in the whole city. No one will think, or even dare, to look for you here."

Before Josie could say more, a light went on and the door opened. A handsome man with dark hair, graying at his temples, stood wrapped in a robe in the muted glow of the lamp.

He smiled at the sight of James. "Seamus! What in all that's holy are you doing here at this time of night?" His voice held the lilt of Ireland.

James grimaced. "I'm afraid I need your help, Father Mark."

"And sure, that's what I assumed. Come in, boy, and bring your friends. A more motley group has never been seen at my doorstep and we don't need to give the good wives of the neighborhood something to wag their tongues about."

The priest stood aside and James propelled first Josie then Aden through the doorway and into a cozy kitchen.

Father Mark gestured toward the table in the corner. "Have a seat, then. I'll put the kettle on and you can tell me your story, Seamus. I see you've found yourself a familiar," he added as he busied himself at the stove. "And a boy one for all that, as well." The man shook his head and tsked.

Knowing how most religions felt about witches and familiars, Aden pressed against James. The kitchen and the man in it didn't seem safe anymore.

James pushed him into a chair by the wall and sat next to him. He patted Aden's knee. "Don't worry. Father Mark is more accepting of our kind than many other priests. We're safe here." He glanced at the still-standing Josie. "All of us." He jerked his chin toward the chair opposite him.

Josie frowned but sat and said nothing as they all watched the priest bustle around making and serving tea. When the steaming cups were poured, Father Mark leaned against the counter cradling his own mug.

"Well then, Seamus, let's hear it."

To Aden's surprise, James — whom the priest called Seamus for some reason — launched into a concise, yet unedited recital of what had happened in the last twenty-four hours with regard to the Appletons. Father

Mark listened without interruption and with no obvious disdain of what he was hearing.

James took a break from his story and a loud sip of his tea. "So, we need a safe place to hide Josie. There's no telling who is in on this whole thing with Mrs. Appleton, but Josie says the book he's hidden contains the names of a lot of prominent people. I certainly don't know who to trust in the police department." James stared into his mug with a look of both anger and…hurt, maybe.

The priest sighed. "And a terrible tale that is. I can't say you're wrong. Even I wouldn't trust my superiors in this matter. Men in power are always corruptible, no matter what mantle they wear. Of course I'll hide this young man here. But Mrs. Flanagan does for me on Wednesday so you'll need to figure out what the solution to all of this is before then. She'll find him for sure, and I can't lie to such a good woman about who he is. It's a lucky thing I don't like having a full-time housekeeper underfoot or this scheme of yours wouldn't work at all."

James stood and held his hand out to Father Mark. "Thank you, and I understand."

"Well, I don't." Josie stood up, crossing his arms and glaring at both James and the priest. "Don't you understand who and *what* I am? Your kind doesn't approve of my kind."

Father Mark put his mug on the counter and went to stand in front of Josie. "I do, yes. I could hardly not, given everything James said. But I don't judge. That's for God to do and, frankly, I think he judges your father, stepmother and everyone else involved in this terrible business far more than he would you or any of the other unfortunates crammed into the jails this evening. You're asking for sanctuary and that's what I'm giving you." The man turned to James. "Until Wednesday, mind."

James nodded. "I promise I'll sort this out before then."

"You might want to start with ferreting out information during dinner tomorrow." He glanced out of the window where the first hint of sunrise could be seen. "Or, later today, it seems. Christ, Jesus, I have mass in a few hours." He rubbed his face before grabbing his mug again and gulping down the rest of his drink.

James grimaced. "You're right. I hate it, but you're right." Taking Aden by the hand, he headed for the door. "Oh, and this is Aden. Yes, he's my familiar and yes, he's a boy. Everyone is going to have to get used to that. Let's go home, baby." With that, he took Aden out of the rectory and handed him into the automobile. "We don't have mass because I never go anymore." He yawned loudly. "I could use a few hours of sleep, though."

Aden took the goggles James handed him and tried not to think about how sleep meant bed and bed meant more than sleep.

* * * *

Despite being exhausted right down to his bones, James couldn't help feeling peppy in one area of his body as he led Aden up to their apartment. When he opened the door, the sight of the bed sent a spark of renewed vigor right to his dick. He dropped his pack, grabbed Aden and hugged him tightly. He couldn't help being rock hard and there was no way to hide his state from his familiar given that their groins were plastered against one another.

James kissed the side of the boy's head. "I was so scared." He hadn't meant to say that, yet the words tumbled out of their own volition.

Aden's small hands clasped his waist and when he spoke, his lips were against James' shoulder. "Were you? It didn't show. You were so in control."

James pulled back enough to look Aden in the eye. "I had to be to keep you safe." Thoughts of what might have happened to his familiar caused his heart to skip a beat. He pulled the boy into another tight hug.

"It wasn't supposed to be like this. Finding people and things for money is just a business for seeker witches. We aren't cops, or soldiers or spies, at least that's not a choice most of us would make. When I picked you as my familiar, it was never with the intention of putting you in harm's way. God, baby, when I think of where you could be right now, it makes me sick to my stomach and my knees weak. In fact, I need to sit down."

James picked up Aden and sat on the bed with the familiar on his lap. Maybe it was the heightened emotions of the night finally getting to him or perhaps he'd realized that having a familiar meant forming a real bond, but whatever it was, James gave in to the temptation to kiss the boy. Aden jerked at the first touch of their lips, then melted into James' embrace and yielded to his touch.

At first, James kept the kiss light, sliding his lips over Aden's. It was almost chaste. Then he got a taste of the boy and smelled his sweet breath. He lost control and pressed his tongue inside Aden's mouth, sweeping every corner and nearly devouring him. He had them lying on the bed without thought, his hands roaming everywhere. The smock was dealt with, interrupting the kiss for only the blink of an eye. His hands found smooth skin to skim, and wandered down to cup Aden's rump without a single thought of what he was doing. It all felt so good, so right, and pressed between their bodies was the familiar's slender cock, hard and just begging to be touched.

James stopped worrying about how to please another man and simply gave in to the urge to clasp the shaft and pump it. Aden moaned and whimpered, bucking into James' fist and digging his fingers into James' shoulder. A cry rang down James' throat as warm cum spurted over his hand. He pumped until Aden stopped shuddering and went lax in his hold.

James ached with need. Rearing away from Aden, he yanked off his own clothing, taking little care as to where he tossed everything and freeing his dick. The cool air of the dawn permeated the room and soothed his overheated skin. He positioned the limp familiar onto his back and settled between the boy's legs. The mere sight of what he'd risked for some filthy lucre of the wealthy enraged him. He needed to release the pent-up emotions and all he could think of was sinking himself deep inside his familiar. Grabbing the lubricant from his nightstand, he slicked up his cock with a thick coating. Then he bent Aden's legs and raised them so that they dangled off his hunched shoulders. The boy's hole still spasmed from his orgasm and the urge to bury his cock was nearly overwhelming. Instead, he held on to the last bit of his control and eased a couple of fingers inside Aden's channel. For the first time, he found the entrance pliable and welcoming. That was all the invitation he needed.

Gripping the backs of Aden's knees, he shuffled forward to position his cock against the familiar's hole. With one thrust, he buried himself balls deep. Aden cried out and arched his back at the sudden invasion, but his cock jerked and swelled, as well. And he squeezed James' dick while bucking his hips in an obvious plea to be fucked. James didn't disappoint either of them. He pulled out until only the head of his dick remained inside before surging forward again. He repeated the motion until he couldn't hold back any longer. It took no time at all for him to come with a bellow that let out his frustration, fury and intense pleasure, all rolled into one sound.

James fucked Aden's ass until they both were wrung dry then, easing out, he collapsed beside his familiar. Taking the boy in his arms, he dropped into sleep.

* * * *

James woke as the sun was well-risen and heading for the peak of the sky. He didn't allow himself to feel guilty, however, given the harrowing night he'd spent. His blood started to boil as he relived the treachery of his first client and how it had brought Aden into unpardonable danger. Still, it had ended well, with Josie tucked up safe and a very pleasurable experience with his familiar in bed. The memory of it had his dick rising. It had help in the form of Aden standing by the stove wearing his union suit. His small rump wiggled as he added bacon to a sizzling frying pan. Too tempting a sight, given that James didn't want to impose too much upon the boy.

Clamping down his burgeoning arousal, he slipped out of bed to relieve himself. He returned to join Aden in the kitchen area. Before he'd even arrived, the familiar was pouring a mug of coffee.

Aden turned to him and offered a shy smile. "Good morning. I hope you don't mind my getting started on breakfast." He frowned. "Or maybe it's too late to call it that. Anyway, I figured you'd want to eat when you woke."

James took the mug, but before taking a sip gave in to the impulse to lean down and plant a kiss on Aden's rosy lips. "The coffee and food are much appreciated. We can't eat too much, though, because we'll be having dinner with my family in a few hours."

The thought of the standing commitment of eating his mother's roast chicken dinner on Sunday afternoon made his stomach tighten. It had become awkward at the best of times since he'd left the force. Bringing his new familiar was going to add to the tension, especially given that Aden was male. His parents had never been totally comfortable with his being a witch, although his father had liked the idea that he could provide extra service to the police. It had given him a certain amount of bragging rights when he'd drunk with his buddies at the local pub. After the scandal of James being kicked out, he imagined his father had weathered a few verbal jabs over it. Now, his abilities were rarely mentioned and there was a certain frosty silence around it with every visit.

Can't be helped.

Aden turned the bacon over and cracked a few eggs in the pan. "I'm going with you?"

James slurped down some coffee, appreciating that Aden made it better than he ever did. "Of course, baby. You're part of the family now."

Aden gave him the side-eye. "I can't imagine they'll be pleased that you picked me. I mean, they must have expected you'd bond with a girl."

"I don't know. We never discussed it." He drained his mug and set it down. "It doesn't really matter what they think because you're mine now and I couldn't be happier with my choice." He hesitated before blurting out the question that had plagued him since waking. "Was last night okay for you? I mean after we returned here."

Aden's cheeks pinked adorably. "More than, thank you."

"No, thank you." James lifted Aden by his shoulders and kissed him lavishly before setting him down again. "I'm going to dress and get a newspaper."

He made short work of his toilette and bounded down the stairs to find his usual newsboy. Once in hand, he scanned the pages for anything about the raid. He found a small article tucked way in the back that said little more than that there had been a raid in Freaktown and the police commissioner was quoted as saying *"to remind the residents in that part of town that no one was above the law."*

James snorted. *Yeah, right. Nothing to see here, people. Move along.*

He returned to the apartment just as Aden was plating their meal. After they had consumed a fair amount, he felt fortified enough to give his familiar the lowdown on his family. Forewarned was forearmed, after all.

James went to refill his mug a second time. "So, putting aside the dozens of aunts, uncles and cousins roaming the streets of Boston, my family consists of four people." He returned to the table and sat. "My father, my mother, my older brother and younger sister."

He took another bite of his food as he considered how much detail to dump on Aden this soon. "Pa was on the force until some years ago when he and a criminal he was struggling with fell down some stairs. He broke his leg very badly and had to retire. He hasn't worked a day since and still walks with a limp."

"That's terrible. Poor man." Aden had a mug of coffee, too, although he'd added so much cream into it, it was more of a coffee-flavored drink.

"Bitter man," James corrected. "He could do something else for a living but considers it beneath him. He's a copper and that's that."

"How does he support his family?" The boy held up his hand. "Sorry, that's none of my business."

James took hold of that hand. "But it is, baby. If for no other reason than I slip some money to Ma whenever I can. She's not too proud to take it, even if Pa is." Letting go, he sat back. "He doesn't mind that she works as a part-time housekeeper to spinster sisters in the Back Bay." He couldn't keep the disapproval out of his voice. "As if she doesn't have enough to do keeping her own house. Anyway, please don't worry about anything anyone says. Fighting at the dinner table is practically required in the Byrne household. My brother is still on the force and Pa has contacts so I'm hoping to learn something more about last night's raid and how Mrs. Appleton figures into all of this."

Aden was quiet for a while, then visibly worked up courage to ask what was on his mind. "What will you do with what you learn? I mean, what's the plan?"

James heaved a sigh. "That, baby, is an excellent question. I'll let you know as soon as I figure it out."

He hoped inspiration would hit him soon because they didn't have much time.

* * * *

Aden looked up at the row house that contained his witch's family. The street was clearly a poor section of South Boston, yet the houses and yards were well-maintained and pretty window boxes offset the obvious age of the buildings. Children wearing what must be their Sunday best played on the street, heedless of the scolding they'd receive for getting dirt on their clothes. James' automobile caught a lot of attention, and he flipped a coin at the oldest boy in exchange for keeping the others off the vehicle.

Aden also garnered some wide-eyed staring. For the first time, he felt self-conscious of how he was dressed. He hoped his new clothes would be ready before the next time he came to this house. Fingering the sides of his smock, he followed James up the stoop and was surprised when he simply walked into the ground floor apartment, using a key from his pocket.

"It's still my home," he said, as if knowing what Aden was thinking. "It's me, Ma!"

Delicious scents of roasted meat hit Aden's nostrils, making them flair and urging him to shift. He tamped that down as the Academy had taught him to do. Being in James' family home meant being as docile as possible. He mustn't do anything to embarrass his witch and he'd savor the roasted chicken and everything else just as much in human form. The apartment was fairly spacious, with an open living and dining area and a hallway leading to more rooms. The kitchen could be seen readily enough beyond the dining table. Everything was clean and neat as a pin, although the furniture and drapes had seen better days. The Byrne family wasn't rich by any standards, yet Mrs. Byrne obviously took pride in her home and made the best with what she had.

The woman herself came bustling over to accept James' kiss on her cheek. "I was wondering if you'd be coming today." Her voice held an Irish lilt.

"Why wouldn't I, Ma?"

The woman narrowed her gaze at Aden. "And sure, one hears things, don't you know."

James chuckled. "Of course. Gossip is currency in this city." He tugged Aden closer. "This is Aden, everyone. My familiar. He's a snow leopard."

Now there were four sets of eyes on him. The father sat in a wing-backed chair by the unlit fireplace while a younger version of the man stood nearby. A pretty girl came from the kitchen, wiping her hands on a dishcloth. She was the only one smiling and she sidestepped her mother to give James a peck on his cheek. Then, to Aden's utter surprise, she came around to do the same for him and winked before returning to the kitchen.

"So, Seamus, are you looking to embarrass us some more?" The provocative question came from the father.

James' mouth tightened only slightly before he shot the man a grin. "I'm only looking to make a living, Pa, and Aden has already proved invaluable in that regard. And please remember I prefer to be called James. I'm an American, after all."

The old man waved his hand in disgust. "Not in my house you're not."

Mrs. Byrne fluttered her hands. "Now, Lorcan, it's Sunday and the Lord wants us to have a peaceful dinner. Come and sit, everyone."

Another place had to be set for Aden because apparently James, not Seamus, hadn't given his family any warning about their new family member coming. He sat gingerly next to James and waited for Mrs. Byrne to give a thankful prayer before helping himself to the food. Actually, it was James who did most of the work, sliding tender pieces of chicken onto his plate, as well as roasted potatoes and carrots. He accepted a glass of lemonade from James' sister.

"Thank you."

She beamed at him. "I'm Mary Kathleen. Everyone calls me Kitty. I don't suppose James bothered to give you that information."

"No, ma'am." Aden looked down and picked up his fork.

Kitty giggled. "No need for formality. You're family now, after all."

"Who says," Mr. Byrne muttered.

"Lorcan, please." Mrs. Byrne turned her gaze to Aden. "Where would you be from, then, Aden?"

"New Haven, Connecticut, ma'am." He was pretty sure that was the right way to address the woman. There was no way he'd be invited to use her given name.

Mrs. Byrne frowned. "No, I mean where do your people come from? Somewhere foreign, I suspect, from the look of you."

"Foreign like Ireland?" James offered with a grin.

"I'm of Tibetan ancestry," Aden jumped to say before he became the cause of a row between his witch and his parents.

"Never heard of it. You're making it up." This from the brother, who sat opposite James and hadn't stopped scowling even as he shoveled food in his mouth.

James patted Aden's arm before responding. "My familiar doesn't lie. Tibet is near China and India. Even you have heard of those countries. You could look it up in an atlas if you ever went to the library."

"I have some news." Kitty practically shouted it to get everyone's attention. When everyone looked her way, she appeared uncertain of what she wanted to say. She licked her lips and flashed her gaze between her parents.

Her father gestured with his fork. "Well, what is it? Don't tell us you've finally landed yourself a beau."

Kitty wrinkled her nose. "No. I've been accepted into the Boston University School of Medicine for this fall."

There was a moment of dead silence before her parents and older brother erupted into various and competing admonishments about her plans. Only James stayed above the fray, eating as if nothing were going on. Aden followed his lead.

Finally, Mr. Byrne slammed a fist on the table, shutting everyone else up. "I'll not have it, my girl. Do you hear me? I let those meddling Lowell sisters talk me into your going to that female college. I only agreed because it was on their dime, but this is too much."

Kitty raised her chin. "Smith College gave me an excellent education and encouraged me to become a doctor. The sisters are willing to pay my tuition again."

"I don't care. I'm your father and I say no."

Mrs. Byrne was more politic. "Kitty, if it's a job you're after, there are plenty for a girl like you, places where you can meet a nice man and settle down. You're long past the age for marriage and children." She tsked. "What good is going to medical school when you'll only have to give it up?"

"I intend to become a doctor, Ma, whether I marry or not." She turned to her father. "And I'm twenty-two. You can't stop me from doing what I want."

"The cheek of it! You'll do as I say or you can't live under my roof."

Kitty daintily wiped her mouth and stood. "Very well. I'll move out." She looked at James. "I don't suppose you have room for me?"

"Sorry. My apartment is only one room and Aden lives there now."

Aden felt his cheeks warm at the implications of James' words. He quickly stuffed the rest of his food in his mouth, sensing that the family dinner was going to be quickly over.

"That's all right. I understand. Miss Amelia and Miss Hester have offered me a place in their home. Naturally I'll pick up my maid duties again to offset their generosity."

"I should never have brought you there to help me. Saints preserve us, this is a terrible thing." Mrs. Byrne looked ready to cry.

"I'm sorry you feel that way, Ma. Now if you'll excuse me, I'm going to pack. James, is it possible for you to give me a ride to the Sisters' house?"

James grinned and sat back, his plate empty. "Sure thing. That's how we refer to them," he told Aden. "They pretty much act as one person, so we think of them as such."

"Thank you." The girl rushed away with her mother hot on her heels, entreating her to change her mind.

James waited until a door slammed shut before saying. "Okay, now that the women have left unexpectedly early, I have some questions for you, Pa, Liam, about the raid last night in Freaktown."

Mr. Byrne took a long drink of his beer. "Why am I not surprised?"

Chapter Six

As sad as he was for Kitty being booted out of the house, James was grateful to have an opening to talk to his father and brother sooner rather than later. Both men were eyeing him with suspicion, and no surprise there. Surely word had trickled through to them that a witch had been involved in some manner.

He decided to be blunt, although not in a way that directly related to the raid, at least from his family's point of view. "What can you tell me about Robert Appleton?"

His father's expression told him he wasn't expecting that question. His brother, however, didn't appear to be surprised. *Interesting*.

"He's a vicious son-of-a-bitch who's not to be trifled with, Seamus." His father was never going to honor his wish to be called James.

"This much I know, Pa. Is it true that he made his fortune blackmailing other men about their dirty little secrets?"

Pa drank some beer, no doubt to give himself time to decide how to answer. He shrugged. "There's been some talk of that. Rich men's business. Not mine. Not that of anyone at this table."

"Sure, Pa. Why would current and former coppers care about the law being broken?"

Pa jabbed a finger in his face. "I never sat upon a horse as high as yours. If you'd kept your head down, you'd still be on the force."

"Yes, but at what price? My honor?"

"Bah!" Pa flicked his hand and stomped into the kitchen as much as his game leg permitted, no doubt to get himself another beer. With the two women unavailable to wait on him, he had to make do.

With his father an obvious dead end, he concentrated on Liam. "What can you tell me?"

"You're such a *bastard*, James." He sneered yet didn't storm off. "Why can't you keep your nose where it belongs?"

"Because powerful people keep dragging me into their messes. If the Commissioner hadn't lied to me to find that man's mistress, I'd still be on the force. And if Melinda Appleton hadn't hired me to find her stepson so that his poor, dying father could see him one last time, I wouldn't have been forced to flee that very conveniently timed raid."

Liam twirled his glass thoughtfully. "I'd heard Appleton was at death's door." He picked up the glass to drain it. "Everyone knows how he made his millions, too."

"I didn't."

"Everyone with a modicum of ambition, and few morals, knows," he amended with a smirk.

Keeping one eye on his father's movements as the man went to sit by the cold fireplace, James leaned across the table to keep the conversation as private as possible.

"All right, Liam. We'll agree that I'm either too righteous or too stupid to have known what was happening in this city. I'm in the shit now, so I need information to pull myself out of it." He flicked his gaze at Aden. "We both know that if I'd been caught last night in the raid, things would have gotten hairy before I got out of it again."

He tried not to think of how Aden would have been treated at the hands of his former-fellow cops. Witch and familiar notwithstanding, the boys would have seen a pretty boy who liked men. The mere thought of how he might have been abused infuriated him, a good reaction because it fueled his questions in a way his brother could not ignore.

"I need more information before I confront Mrs. Appleton."

Liam raised his eyebrows. "Christ, Jesus, you're a prig. Do you really think you can confront such a powerful woman? And where, in her own home?" He shook his head. "You won't even get past whatever servant opens the door. And if you try to force your way in, you'll only get yourself arrested after all. Face it, brother. You were used as a stalking horse and I'm sure paid handsomely for it. Get out while the getting's good and be thankful it didn't end worse for you."

James could feel Aden's gaze on him. He didn't dare look at the familiar because he knew what he was thinking. "I can't let it go because it's not over. Mrs. Appleton and whomever she has in her pocket aren't going to leave me be."

Liam sighed heavily. "Fuck me. You know where the Appleton boy is."

"Perhaps," James equivocated. "They undoubtedly think I do. I need to speak with Mrs. Appleton. She's cold and calculating but I don't think she has much spine. Maybe we can come to some agreement." He drummed his fingers on the arm of his chair. "I need to figure out a place outside her home where I can spring on her."

"Well, now, she's a very social person. There may be some do or other that rich people like to go to, although how you'd wrangle your way in, I can't imagine."

James' heart sank. His brother was right. The rich went to great lengths to keep the riffraff out of their social gatherings. Other than servants, of course, but there was no way for him to finesse into that kind of job. He'd have to try to somehow — if he could even figure out where she might be. There wasn't much time, either, before Father Mark would need Josie out of the rectory.

"There must be something in the paper about an event. There's a society page, isn't there? A gossip column?"

"And sure there is, brother. After the bloody thing has happened."

"There must be a way to find out in advance. Who can I ask?" The answer came to him at the same moment as Liam. "The Sisters," they said in unison and, for a moment, it was like they were children again, close confidants.

Liam just had to kill the mood. "That means talking to them. Good luck with that."

* * * *

Aden wasn't sure how to feel about having a pretty young woman perched on his lap with her arms flung around his neck. No one had ever done so in his entire life and it gave him an uneasy sense of responsibility for her safety. James wasn't driving very fast, but Kitty still squealed each time he took a corner and tightened her grip around his neck. Aden had given her his goggles, which seemed the right thing to do, but that meant he had to make the journey with his eyes closed against the wind and dust. A pleasant smell of lavender permeated his nostrils and her body was soft where James' was hard. It caused a distant memory of his mother to rise, one of comfort. If most men would have found the position provocative, he found it awkward. Her presence meant he had more than his own body to keep safely in the automobile instead of falling into the street. And with her carpet bag wedged between his feet, the was no way for him to move even his legs to find purchase on his seat. So he held onto the edge of it while wrapping an arm gingerly around Kitty's waist.

James slowed down, then stopped. Aden opened his eyes to the lovely sight of a row of tall townhouses, rising up from the street like a line of soldiers at the ready. Lush gardens spilled out of the small front yards, but there was no sign of laundry lines or kids playing in the street. Here only families in their Sunday best strolled around, mothers pushing prams and fathers holding the hands of older children. A beat cop sauntered down the street, hands behind his back, smiling and tipping his hat to those he passed. The neighborhood was so different from the one the Byrnes lived in, it was a different world, as different as Freaktown was.

James hopped out and came around to help his sister off Aden's lap. It was a relief to be free of the weight and the responsibility. Once James had the carpet bag in hand, Aden was able to jump off himself. He stood staring up at the five-story home and marveled at how women living in such luxury could care enough about a poor Irish girl's education. It was charity, he supposed, and something to do to alleviate what had to be otherwise boring lives. What did wealthy women do all day, given that they weren't permitted to work outside the home and had servants to tend to that which needed doing inside?

He followed Kitty and James through the wrought-iron gate and around the side of the house. Kitty knocked on the back door. She seemed a bit sad, although he didn't know her well enough to say for sure. It was terrible being ejected out of your family home. He understood that all too well. A few seconds later, the door was opened by a young woman around Kitty's age whose skin was the color of his, coffee and cream. Her pretty, broad face lit up.

"Kitty, we weren't expecting you!" She grabbed the woman by the hand and practically pulled her inside. "Look, everyone. It's Kitty."

James and Aden trotted after them, stepping into a kitchen that was bigger than James' entire apartment. A round, white-haired woman stepped away from the stove, wiping her hands on her apron, and greeted Kitty with the same enthusiasm. Two men, one older and one younger, stood from the table to greet James' sister. The girl was certainly well liked in this household.

"Now, why would you be coming in the servants' entrance, I want to know." The cook's Irish accent was even thicker than that of Mr. and Mrs. Byrne.

Kitty glanced at James before answering. Her eyes glistened with unshed tears. "Because, Mrs. McCarthy, my father has kicked me out and now I have to live here as a servant again while I go to medical school. I mean, it's not like I'll be a guest."

"And sure and why not?" The cook shook her head. "The mistresses think of you as a niece, don't you know. I'll fix up the bedroom on the third floor."

Kitty reached out as if to grab the woman's arm. "No, please don't. I just need to talk to the Sisters and let them know I have to take up their generous offer once again. Are they in the front parlor?"

Aden was pondering how there could be more than one parlor in the house when James interjected.

"I'd like to see them, too." He cleared his throat. "You know, as Kitty's male relative, I need to be sure of her arrangements."

Kitty barked out a laugh. "Go on and pull the other one. You've done your brotherly duty and seen me safely here and I thank you, but there's no need for you to stay."

"There's every need, Mary Kathleen," James insisted with clenched teeth.

Something in his expression must have gotten through to his sister because she simply nodded. "Maizy, would you please see if they'll receive us?"

The maid hurried from the room with a smile and was back in under a minute. "They say you're all to come to the parlor and would Cook please bring in some tea for our guests."

Kitty turned to the cook. "That's not necessary, Mrs. McCarthy."

The woman raised an eyebrow. "If you think not, feel free to argue your case with the mistresses." With that, she hustled back to the stove.

Kitty grimaced at her brother. "Come on, then." As they walked into the hallway, she leaned in closer to his ear. "You better not be doing anything to hurt my position here."

"Not to worry, little sister. I merely want to ask them a favor."

"Jesus wept, that's what I'm afraid of."

There was no more time for talking as they entered a beautiful room that managed to look cozy as well. The Lowell sisters were elderly women who looked nothing alike. One was tall and thin with a sharp face and the other was shorter and plumper. Both were white-haired and simply, yet elegantly, dressed and adorned. When Kitty entered, they greeted her as if she were a long-lost daughter. The obvious affection and open welcome put Aden at ease. These women were nothing like the Melinda Appletons of the world.

Kitty pulled away from their embrace. "Miss Hester and Miss Amelia, I'd like to introduce you to my brother, James."

"Oh, the witch!" the shorter woman cried out with glee. She looked at Aden. "And his familiar?" She peered closely at him. "What kind of animal are you, dear boy?"

Aden twisted his fingers in front of him. "Um, a snow leopard, ma'am."

The woman actually clapped her hands. "Did you hear that, Hester? How wonderful. Would you do us the honor of changing?" She looked at James. "Oh, I suppose I should ask you?"

James smiled broadly. "Not at all, ma'am. Aden is free to shift whenever he likes." He gave Aden an encouraging nod and caught the smock as it slipped off Aden's animal body.

Ignoring the twin squeals and the human chatter that followed as the Bryne siblings made themselves comfortable, Aden scented his surroundings. There were so many overlapping smells — the remnants of dinner, notes of various flora, and the strange humans — he didn't really pay much attention to what the humans were saying until he heard James speak the name Appleton. He went to sit by James' side and focused on the conversation.

Miss Amelia wrinkled her button-like nose. "Sister and I try not to socialize with that family. There's something distasteful about Robert and his, um, dare I say gold-digger wife."

Hester's back went ridgid. "Sister, we don't make such judgments. They are beneath us."

"But, sister," Amelia huffed. "You know it's true."

"Be that as it may. Ah, here's Maizy with the tea."

James declined for both of them when offered a cup. Kitty sat ramrod straight in a chair on the other side of James, clearly unhappy with the topic.

Hester sniffed. "There is indeed something distasteful about that couple, even though the Appletons are an old Boston Family."

"You are being too kind, sister." Amelia beamed at Aden. "Oh, would you like a saucer of cream?"

"Really, sister. He's not a cat."

"He's a kind of cat. Does he like cream?" she asked of James.

"Only in his coffee, ma'am."

The Lowell sisters both twittered at that. James laid a hand on Aden's head and stroked it. Aden couldn't help purring at the pleasure of it. That set their hosts into a short ecstasy of delight. They talked over each other and peppered both Kitty and James with questions about how their parents had taken the news about Kitty's education.

With a big sigh, Hester put down her teacup. "Such a shame, my dear. But of course, you must live here while you study. We know you'll do great things, Kitty."

"Thank you, Miss Hester. I'll help Maizy with the cleaning to earn my keep."

Miss Ameilia gasped. "Oh no, my dear. You are our guest. And you must spend all of your time and energy on your studies. We insist. Don't we, sister?"

Hester nodded, her face serious. "We do. Sister and I would have loved to have gone to college, but there was nowhere for us to go. And Pappa insisted we marry someone suitable as soon as we had our coming outs. We didn't like any of his choices."

"No, indeed. Frightful, every one of them. Better to become spinsters than be tied to such boring, insufferable men."

"Well said, sister. Well said. So you see, Kitty, it's all settled. You'll live with us and become a doctor and go out into the world and do all the things we never could."

Kitty beamed. "I promise I'll make the most of this opportunity. I can't ever repay you for your generosity."

"We don't need you to," Hester said. "We have plenty of money. Don't we, sister?"

"My yes, buckets."

The sisters twittered again, obviously happy to have a protégé to focus their attention on."

"She's like a project to them."

It startled Aden to hear his witch's voice in his head. *"They seem to truly like her."*

"Yes, I'm glad to be here to see it for myself but I must get back to business."

"Ladies, I understand you don't like socializing with the Appletons, but it's imperative that I speak with Mrs. Melinda Appleton. I'm hoping to…um, catch her, if you will, at an event outside her home. I was wondering if you might have any idea where and when she might attend one."

The two women looked at each other and said in unison, "Winifred's salon."

"That's our cousin," Hester clarified. "She likes to hold a Boston version of a French salon. You know, an evening filled with interesting people, like artists."

Amelia rolled her eyes. "It's mostly the usual crowd of Boston families. Hardly Paris. Melinda likes to frequent them and Sunday night is her usual time for gatherings."

James' excitement was palpable. He leaned forward. "I don't suppose you could wrangle an invitation for me?"

The Lowell sisters looked at one another and smiled.

Miss Amelia answered. "We'll do better than that. You can escort us. Won't it be delicious to arrive on the arm of such a handsome young man?"

"Very much so, sister. And of course you must come as well, Kitty. We can show you off."

"Oh, thank you, but I don't have anything appropriate to wear."

Ameilia dismissed that with a wave of her hand. "We'll take care of that, don't you worry. And we have some of Pappa's old clothes that should fit you, Mr. Byrne."

James looked down at himself. "I was thinking this would be good enough."

"No." The sisters once again spoke as one.

Amelia turned to Aden. "You, dear boy, should go just as you are. It will cause such a stir."

James cleared his throat. "I was hoping to keep our presence low-key."

"Our father was a naval officer and he taught us strategy because we were the only ones willing to listen. Your familiar will be quite the distraction while you hunt down Melinda." Amelia put her hand to her bosom. "My, this is going to be so exciting. Won't it, sister?"

"Indeed."

And that was how Aden ended up going to his first high society party. He wasn't sure he liked the idea, but his witch needed him to play his part, so he would.

* * * *

James tugged at his collar. The late Commadore Lowell had been a big man, but his shoulders hadn't been as wide as James' and it was hard to be comfortable without worrying he'd bust a seam open. His attire was at least twenty years out of date, not that he cared. The suit was of very fine quality, so he blended in with the silks and superfines of Winifred Lowell Dashwood's coterie. No one gave him more than a cursory look. It was Aden who was garnering all the attention. And no surprise there. The familiar was a vision of sleek beauty. His natural coat of golds and browns would have captured anyone's eye, but the real topper was the ruby necklace Miss Ameilia had fixed around his neck. James had balked at the adornment at first, then accepted that the more attention Aden drew, the better chance James had to pull Melinda in for a private conversation.

Besides, even in leopard form, the pleasure Aden took from being prettied up was enough for James to agree. In the scant couple of days he'd known the boy, James had developed strong feelings for him. It was more than that of a witch protecting his familiar and not quite a big brother need to protect the way he felt about Kitty. This was deeper and not all together comfortable. The physical intimacy, something he had considered a necessary part of his profession, had awakened a need in him that he hadn't realized was there, buried deep. Sex was sex. It made him feel good and helped him get to sleep. He hadn't expected the act to elicit any emotions, at least not yet. Someday, maybe, he assumed he'd find a woman to settle down with and raise a family. How his familiar would fit into that life wasn't something he'd thought about. Now, he couldn't imagine a life without Aden and he wasn't sure he even wanted or needed anything or anyone more.

Miss Hester touched his arm. "There she is, holding court in the corner." The woman made a sour face. "She's always been an outrageous flirt and her husband didn't seem to mind. With him not even here, she is entirely without discretion."

James followed the woman's gaze and yes, there Melinda Appleton stood in the far corner of the large sitting room. Three men of various ages hung on her every word. It took a moment for the murmur of the excited crowd to reach them. When it did, she turned in the direction of other guests' focus and frowned. It was hard to see Aden, crowded as he was by a semicircle of admirers, but she spotted James within seconds. With a narrowed gaze and a frown, she extracted herself from the men and headed for a far doorway. Despite her efforts to saunter as if she were in no hurry, her expression said she was determined to flee.

James wasted no time following her, slipping through the throng of people. No one paid him any mind. He reached what turned out to be a library mere seconds after Melinda disappeared inside it.

"Mrs. Appleton." He didn't have to raise his voice in the relative quiet of the room.

Melinda stiffened, stopped and turned to face him. She snapped open her painted fan and waved it in front of her decolletage where the swell of lovely breasts showed above her scarlet silk gown. Gone was the demure and worried wife of a dying man. Here was a woman who could snag a man with one sultry look.

"Mr. Byrne. What a surprise. I wouldn't have thought a poor boy from South Boston would travel in my social circles. Have you and your familiar dared to sneak into Mrs. Dashwood's salon? Shall I call for footmen to throw you out?"

James matched her false cheer. "No need, Mrs. Appleton. I'm escorting the Lowell sisters. My sister is their protégé and they are quite taken by my familiar."

Melinda's mouth formed a mou. "Someone needs to tell those spinsters that eccentricity has its limits." She made to move past him. "I believe it's time for me to leave. I've grown weary of the company."

James took a sidestep into her path. "Please stay a moment longer. We need to talk."

Melinda managed to stare down her nose at him despite being far shorter. "Do we? About how you've failed to find my stepson after taking my money?"

James bared his teeth. "We both know I found him. It must have been very disappointing to learn he'd slipped the net you'd managed to cast with the police."

"I have no idea what you're talking about." Once again, she tried to move around him.

He countered and brought her up short. "Your lie isn't credible, Mrs. Appleton. A police raid in Freaktown in the very bawdy house where Josie plays piano on the very night I find him?" He shook his head. "It pains me that you used me as a stalking horse. It's not the betrayal, you see, but my failure to realize I was being followed. I'm red-faced with shame, which makes me all the more determined to thwart whatever your plans are. It's a matter of pride as much as a personal code of morality."

Melinda dropped all pretense. "Where is he? I'll double your fee if you tell me." When James merely stared, she upped the ante. "Triple it, then. No?" Her expression turned sultry. "Whatever it is you want, I'll give it to you."

James nearly laughed. "You have nothing I want, ma'am. Except the truth. Who is behind this? As rich as you are through your husband, you don't have his access to the kind of clout one needs to control the police. Someone must be very worried about your husband's book making its way to the newspaper. Or maybe just to the legislators. I'm sure a lot of powerful men want that book, but not all powerful ones are in it. I only want to broker a deal for Josie to be left alone. He has no intention of releasing it to anyone but he fears for his life given what he knows is in it." He took a step closer. "If you were smart, you'd be worried too. I can ensure the safety of both of you. Surely you know you're expendable. There are plenty of young, beautiful women out there. No man needs to curry favor with you to meet his needs."

He saw he'd hit the mark with the flare in her eyes. Melinda did indeed think she could protect herself with her body and her wiles.

There was no chance for her to respond, however. A man strode in, tall and thin with slicked-back blond hair and a fashionable mustache with a hint of red in it. His face was vaguely familiar.

"Is there a problem, Mrs. Appleton?" He sneered at James. "Is this man bothering you?"

When the man was only a few feet away, an invisible spark hit James. It took all his effort not to react, but he could tell the man had felt it too. *He's a witch.*

Melinda regained her composure. "Not at all, Mr. Wyles. Mr. Byrne was just telling me about his familiar. It's creating quite a stir out there and the noise is giving me a headache." She pressed two fingers delicately against her temple. "I need to leave."

"Of course." The man stepped aside to give her a clear path and making it impossible for James to impede her.

Melinda sailed out of the room like a queen, whatever doubts he'd sowed in her no longer showing.

Wyles glared at him. "Do you know who I am?"

"Should I?" The man looked comfortable in the milieu of the wealthy, yet something about him didn't quite fit in.

"I'm Mayor Adams' personal secretary. And Mrs. Appleton is a particular friend of his. Naturally, I am duty-bound to protect her."

Interesting. He supposed Wyles held a coveted position, but even so, it made no sense to him that he'd be invited to such a soirée. Not that there was any point in saying as much. He chose to shove his curiosity aside and deal with what was in front of him.

"She doesn't need protecting from me. I am not a man who preys on women."

Wyles' lip curled. "Your reputation precedes you, Mr. Byrne. I'm aware that you have a...code that you adhere to even when it's not in your best interests. I would have thought your boundaries would extend to someone like Mrs. Appleton. She is a genteel woman and under tremendous strain, given her husband's state of health."

"She's about to lose her meal-ticket, I'll give you that."

Wyles took a step toward him, fingers clenched and arm half raised. He visibly worked to control himself. "You, sir, are no gentleman, and you've worn out your welcome here. I suggest you leave and take that mangy familiar with you."

James knew when he was being goaded and also understood when discretion was the better part of valor. Besides, the insult to both him and Aden was laughably untrue.

"I've tired of this soirée indeed. Good night, sir."

He left the library more than pleased that he'd at least put a bee in Melinda's bonnet. It had been too much to hope for that she'd give him the information he needed. Best to retreat and consider his next steps. Besides, he was beginning to resent all the attention others were paying to his familiar. He wanted the boy all to himself and was eager to get him home.

Chapter Seven

Despite the fact that James was bone-tired after the long and mostly frustrating day, he was eager to get home and enjoy some time with Aden. The familiar was back in human form, wearing that sack of clothing that James was starting to loathe. Someone so beautiful should be able to show it off. He couldn't wait to get the boy's new clothes. Perhaps he could pay for them to be done earlier. He was a little more flush thanks to Melinda, the one good thing to come out of all this craziness. There was no reason he couldn't splurge a little on his new family member.

James turned to smile at the boy as they arrived at his stoop. He didn't see his assailant, but knew something was wrong from the look of alarm crossing Aden's face. The next thing he saw was stars as a fist plowed into his jaw. He staggered and came back swinging even as another man rushed up from behind to grab him in a bear hug. A second blow had him doubling over, but the third one never landed. With a throaty growl, Aden in leopard form sprang onto the first man's back and sank his teeth in his shoulder. An ungodly shriek rent the air as the man twirled to dislodge the big cat. Aden held on with one paw and slashed the man's chest with the other.

James took this all in even while he hooked his foot behind his assailant's and managed to flip both of them to the ground. The band around his chest eased, giving him the chance to turn to face his attacker and deliver an uppercut. The man turned out to have a jaw like a pillow. His eyes rolled back into his head and he sprawled in the muddy street. Taking no chances, James kicked him in the side and knew a moment of great satisfaction when he heard something crack.

He whirled around to find and help Aden. All he saw was the first man fleeing the scene, holding a hand to his neck and with no care for his companion. Aden crouched on the banister. His muzzle was bloody but he appeared otherwise unharmed. James let out a breath he hadn't realized he was holding. Then he went to make use of the man who remained behind. He bent down and hauled the barely conscious man to his feet.

James shook him by his lapels. "Wakey, wakey, asshole. We need to have a talk."

When nothing coherent came out of the man, James dragged him to the stoop and, sitting him down, slapped his cheeks to bring him more fully around.

James peered into his eyes. "Do you see me, boyo? I want answers. Come on, pull it together or I'll give my familiar a go at you."

That threat got the guy's attention. He stared glassy-eyed at James. "I got nothing to say."

"Ah, now we both know that's a lie. Who set you on me?" When the man didn't answer, James jerked his head in Aden's direction. "Once my familiar's tasted blood, he craves more. I don't think I'm inclined to rein him in."

It was a lie, of course. He knew nothing of the sort about Aden, although, at a guess, he didn't think the boy had it in him to be vicious. Well, not too much so. He also wouldn't allow the familiar to do anything that would get him into trouble with the law. The neighborhood might be quiet at the moment but he was certain people were looking from behind their curtains. They'd made too much noise in the fight for folks to miss.

Their attacker knew none of this, of course. And Aden, bless him, was a quick study. He growled at the man, flashing his bright, deadly fangs and looking ready to pounce at the first opportunity.

The guy shrank back. "You keep that beast away from me."

"Give me an incentive to do so. Give me a more worthy target."

A few tense seconds ticked by, then... "Some toff paid us. Said you were bad news and to make sure you got the message."

"And what message was that?"

The man shrugged. "I guess to stop doing whatever it is you're doing that's pissing someone off."

James rocked back on his heels, considering his next question. "This guy who paid you, describe him. Tall with blond hair and a ginger mustache?"

The guy tried to sneer, winced and cupped his jaw. "Nah. Broad and dark-haired. Kind of like you, but shorter."

So, not Wyles. Of course a man like that had underlings to do his dirty work, including paying for others to do the dirtiest work.

He jerked his head. "Get lost and let whoever paid you know I'm no easy mark. And I don't scare easy."

The paid muscle didn't need to be told twice. He rose slowly, holding his arm against what James hoped was at least a cracked rib, and hobbled away.

James waited until he was out of sight before gathering Aden's smock and slippers. "Come on, baby. Let's get inside." He winced himself. Now that the fight was over, he could feel the sting of his split lip and the ache of his own ribs.

Aden bounded up the stoop and waited for James to open the front door. The familiar stayed in animal form until they were safely in their own apartment. Then he shifted and lunged to hug James.

"Are you all right?"

James bit back a grunt. "I'm fine. Nothing's broken."

Aden eased back. "Sorry, I forgot one of those brutes punched you in the stomach." He waved a couple of fingers around James' mouth. "And your poor lip. You're bleeding."

James licked the bit of dried blood that had trickled down. "Nothing I haven't had before." He peered at the boy. "You've got blood on your mouth, too."

Aden went into the bathroom. "It's not mine. Shifting doesn't always get everything off me. I'll wash it. Sit down and take your shirt off." Water started running.

James was all too happy to comply. Dropping Aden's things, he sat heavily on the side of the bed and peeled off his jacket and waistcoat. He was damn glad to have changed back into his own clothes, even though the Lowell sisters had tried to get him to keep their father's things. He didn't like to think how hampered he would have been fighting in the tight formal-wear. Easing his shirt off, he grimaced at the already-blooming bruise on his lower ribcage.

"Oh my God!" Aden came running toward him with a wet cloth. "Are you sure nothing's broken?"

James was momentarily tongue-tied because the vision of a naked Aden was a great distraction from his aches and pains. He grabbed the boy by the waist and brought him in between his legs. But when he tried to set the boy down on his lap, his ribs protested too loudly for him to ignore. He winced and let Aden go.

"Damnation! It hurts like a bitch. You're going to have to do all the work tonight, baby."

Aden furrowed his brow. "Work?" He raised the cloth and gently dabbed at the corner of James' mouth.

"In bed."

Aden scoffed. "Sex? How can you think about that with these injuries?"

"How can I not with you standing there tempting me?"

"Tempting?" Aden scowled. "What nonsense."

Only a few days ago, James would have agreed. No more. He cupped both cheeks of Aden's adorable backside and pulled him in against his crotch. "Can you feel what you do to me?" He rubbed their bodies together, ignoring his ribs' protest.

Aden pushed against James' shoulders to pull back, but James held on firmly.

"You're in no condition for such activity. Let me tend you and I'll draw you a bath to soothe your aches."

"Nothing aches more than my dick, baby. It strongly disagrees with you about what I'm fit for."

"James."

"Aden." He slid one hand up to clasp the back of the familiar's neck to bring his face down for a kiss.

Aden didn't resist, much, but when their lips touched, it was impossible to stop the hiss from escaping.

"*See.*"

A wicked idea entered James' head that he couldn't resist. "My mouth may be injured but yours isn't." He pressed on the boy's shoulders. "Down on your knees, baby. Please," he added because maybe this wasn't something Aden knew about or wanted to do.

The familiar didn't resist. With the grace of his animal spirit, he sank down between James' legs. He tossed the cloth on the floor and reached up to the fly of James' pants. He made short work of opening it, freeing the cock that was fully erect and dying to come out and play.

Aden peered up at him from under his lashes. "Do you want me to take you into my mouth?"

"God yes. But only if you want to do it. This isn't really about strengthening our bond."

"Does everything we do have to be?" Aden licked his lips in an innocent provocation. "I mean, can't we enjoy each other just for the sake of having fun?"

James' dick twitch in response. "We can. I want to. Do you?"

By way of an answer, the boy licked his lips again and opened his mouth wide. The moment James' cockhead entered that warm, tight place, he groaned with intense pleasure. Women had done this for him a few times, those who were bold in their interests. This was different. Somehow. Some way. Everything with his familiar was new and exciting. The familiar braced himself with both hands on James' thighs. The feel of his small fingers pressed into his skin gave him an added boost of desire.

His brain winked out as Aden slid his tongue around James' shaft. With his eyes closed, he concentrated on the delicious feel of his cock being licked and sucked like the candy on a stick he'd enjoyed as a treasured treat. He carded his fingers through the strands of the familiar's hair and clenched them in a tight grip. The urge to push Aden's head down was strong and he gave in to it only for a second. The sounds of his familiar choking forced him to ease up. It was harder than he would have expected to exert such control, but the last thing he wanted was to make this experience a chore for his boy. Sex of any kind between them had to be based on mutual agreement and trust.

James wanted to savor the blow job. His balls had other ideas. On a particularly hard suck, they exploded. He didn't even have time to warn Aden that he was coming before his cum filled the boy's mouth. Instead of pulling away, Aden leaned over to take James' dick a little farther in and swallow the cum with quick gulps. The way the familiar's fingers dug into James' flesh caused a final spurt even as he thought he'd shuddered his last from the orgasm. When he was bone dry, he collapsed back onto the bed.

Aden pressed his face to the side of James' groin. "Did I do that right?"

James barked out a laugh. "Any righter and you'd have killed me." Ignoring the protest of his ribs, he sat up and cupped Aden's head to kiss him.

It didn't matter that his split lip stung. He wanted to show his appreciation. He could taste his own spending that lingered in the boy's mouth. It should have been disgusting, yet it wasn't. The mingling of their flavors brought a sense of intimacy that surpassed that which came from fucking. His witch power flared inside him. Aden's emotions mingled with his own for the first time. He didn't simply hear the familiar's thoughts, he *felt* them. Nothing he'd ever been told or read about his special condition had mentioned how totally blended he'd become with his familiar.

The sensation was so electrifying, he didn't want the experience to ever stop. It was Aden who found the strength to break the kiss. The boy pulled back and stood up. Then he put distance between them, leaving James sitting on the edge of the bed with his dick already rallying for more.

A bit confused and disappointed, James stared at Aden. "Didn't you feel that, baby? Didn't you like the feeling of…being so close?"

Aden's cheeks turned bright pink in an instant and his eyes glistened as if tears threatened. "I…I loved it. I love *you*, James. That's not what is supposed to happen." The poor boy sounded not just confused but distraught.

James had to shove aside the flash of joy at his familiar's declaration of love. Something was wrong and it was his responsibility to figure out what.

"What did you expect for things to be like between us?" he asked in a gentle tone.

Aden shrugged. "Duty. Mine is to be your helpmate, boost your power, obey your commands. And in return, you'd take care of me. Keep me safe from other witches and give me as good a life as I could expect as a familiar." Aden pressed his lips shut and looked away.

James bit back a grunt as he stood and went to the boy. He took him gently by the shoulders. "You were told sex was almost a chore, I guess, in order to strengthen our bond."

With his gaze fixed on the floor, Aden nodded. "I was told not to expect to like it, just submit." His eyelashes fluttered and he looked up at James. "It feels as if we're nearly one person and when I look at you, my heart hurts with how much love I have for you. How is that possible? We've known each other for such a short time and we haven't...you know, connected more than a handful of times. Yet, when I took you into my mouth, it was as if you'd invaded my whole body."

James swallowed down a lump filling his throat. "Are you scared or...disgusted?" He held his breath waiting for the answer.

Aden didn't hesitate. He fell into James' embrace. "I'm not afraid. Only surprised. I know my life with you will be wonderful." He paused. "And I understand how it's different for you. I'm a tool for your power. That's okay. I just want to please you."

The familiar's words tugged James' heart. He wanted to say he loved the boy back but wasn't sure that what he felt constituted that delicate emotion. He only knew that the familiar made him whole when he hadn't understood that he was missing a vital piece of himself.

"You are part of me now, baby. Never think that you are merely something useful to me. We are bonded together in a unique way that makes me very happy."

Aden glanced up. "Really?"

"Absolutely. And I'm delighted that cock sucking is something that you enjoyed. You did, didn't you?"

Aden gave him a shy smile. "Oh, yes. Can't you tell?"

He'd been so consumed by the emotions, James hadn't noticed that the familiar was aroused. He did now, and wormed his hand between them to clasp the slender dick. "Let's have a bath and I'll take care of that for you."

"A bath? Together?"

"Together. Always."

* * * *

Aden snuggled against James' hard, warm side. He wanted to hug the man close, but didn't dare for fear of hurting him. The long soak in the tub had brought out the livid bruise where the thug had viciously punched him. Thinking about the attack infuriated Aden. He hadn't realized how mad he could get until the moment when his witch had been punched. Shifting and launching his own attack hadn't taken any thought. He'd reacted out of instinct and, at that moment, he had truly felt his full and true nature. It was a little unnerving how much he'd enjoyed the taste of the man's blood, but he trusted James to keep him in check. A familiar without a witch could be a dangerous thing. He understood that now more than ever.

"Can't sleep?"

The sound of James' voice in the dark startled Aden. He'd thought the man was out for the night after the trying day.

"Sorry, did I wake you?" He wasn't sure how he could have except they were connected very strongly now.

"I can practically hear your brain churning, but no. I can't seem to turn off mine, either."

"Are we any closer to learning how to help Josie? We didn't have a chance for you to tell me how things went with Mrs. Appleton. Not that I'm expecting you to give me more information than you think I should have." He needed to remember that whatever his feelings for James were, the witch was still his master.

James clasped Aden's hand. "You are entitled to know everything I do. This is a partnership, remember?"

The words warmed him so much, he tried to snuggle even closer. "I'll try to. I just trust you to do what's best for us both no matter what."

"I'm humbled by that, baby. And I'm determined to put this situation to bed with everyone safe." He sighed. "But Melinda was no help and she's got a rather rabid protector in the form of the mayor's secretary. I'm afraid I'm going to have to up the ante on this."

"I don't understand what that means.

"In this case, it means I'm going to see my friend, Mike, tomorrow. He works for the newspaper and usually knows everything in this city worth knowing. I have to find leverage somewhere to get Josie out of this mess."

"Okay. May I come with you?" He didn't want to leave James' side for one moment. Another attack could be coming.

"Of course. Where I go, you go, if for no other reason than I don't want to leave you alone and vulnerable."

Aden thought James was the one at greater risk, but didn't say so. Loving his witch didn't change the fact that he was not supposed to question the man.

And yet, there was something that kept teasing his brain.

"May I ask you something?"

"Anything, baby. Always."

Aden marshalled his thoughts for a few seconds. He knew he was going to be treading on sensitive ground. "Everyone keeps mentioning your leaving the police force. It sounds like they think you made some kind of mistake. Even people at the party were whispering about you. Why did you leave? What happened?"

At first, he didn't think James was going to answer. The witch rubbed his thumb along the back of Aden's hand and, as James had said about him, it was as if Aden could see the man's brain working out a problem.

"I'm sorry you had to ask. I should have explained my situation to you from the beginning. It's likely to come up again, so you should understand my perspective on it.

"I'm a seeker witch. Everyone knows that, and has since I entered puberty and started to show the signs. Some witches and their families try to hide and it's easier for us to do so than it is for familiars. I could sense that my parents wanted me to suppress my nature and keep it quiet from others, if only because the Catholic church isn't all that accepting of our kind. I couldn't do it, though. The urge to use my powers was too strong and, well, frankly I was proud to be different, to have an innate skill that could be put to good use.

"One of the very first things I did with my gift was find the Sisters' cat. They were delighted, even though it wasn't very hard to do. Word got around and my father was approached to have me join the force as soon as I was old enough. The fact that his much-beloved police pals wanted me was enough for him to drop all concerns about making my talent public. It was a great job. I loved using my skill to help recover stolen items and find elusive bad guys. I really basked in the admiration of my fellow coppers and my father's pride in me, truth be told. I knew that when I had the chance to get a familiar, my career was really going to take off."

When James fell silent, Aden forced himself to wait. To not force anything by asking questions.

"And then one day, the commissioner of all people called me into his office. I was walking on a cloud when I went in. There was another man, a state senator, as it happens, sitting there. They both greeted me warmly, even with a certain level of comradery that should have rung warning bells for me, but didn't. Men of their station don't usually hold Southie boys like me as their equals. It was a lure because they needed me.

"You see, the senator had a mistress. The man wasn't even shy about saying so. Powerful men get a pass on fidelity, apparently. The young woman had a history of hysteria and she'd taken off on him. He was worried for her, wanted her found so that he could protect her and get her the help that she needed."

Again, James paused. Then he took a big breath and continued.

"He gave me a comb of hers and it didn't take me long to form a connection. I was surprised to realize she was in Freaktown. I didn't want to alarm the man by saying so. Instead, I pretended that I didn't yet have a line on her and asked for time to track her down. She was staying in a brothel of all places, but she wasn't working in it, thank God. She'd found it as a refuge through a network of women in the city.

"She was pregnant." Bitterness dripped from every word.

Aden couldn't help interjecting. "So the senator was worried about his unborn child?"

"No. He was worried she wouldn't have the abortion that he demanded of her. No bastard for him. Not good for his public image. A mistress was tolerated so long as nothing tangible was around to proclaim what he was up to. The poor woman was little more than a child herself. She wanted to keep her baby but knew the senator was too powerful for her to escape his clutches."

"She wasn't hysterical." Aden could see what the man's plan had been, could feel the fury over the situation building in James.

"No, she wasn't. Not the way he described it. Only desperate to keep him from handing her over to a doctor who would rid her of the child and make sure she was never able to get pregnant again. I didn't even know that was possible."

Aden rolled to his side in order to lay his free hand across James' abdomen, careful not to press on his injured ribs. "You helped her get away."

"I did, by throwing the senator off the scent and giving her money and time to go far away from his reach. They found out, of course. Eventually. And oh, such a stink there was. You would have thought I'd committed treason instead of helping a desperate woman whom all decent men would have protected. I was tossed off the force and warned to keep my mouth shut. I agreed on the condition that I was given a…pension."

He sighed again. "Yeah, I took their filthy lucre, gave up on any hope of climbing the ranks of the force and decided it was time to open up a private agency. I was determined not to violate my own moral code. Just my luck that Melinda Appleton managed to put me right back into the same corner."

"And just like the last time, you've done the right thing." Aden stretched to plant a soft kiss on his witch's mouth. "I'm proud of you, James, and honored to be by your side."

James took him by the chin before he could move away. "I've put you at risk, baby. This time, it's not only me that will feel the wrath of powerful men. It's not fair to you, and if you want..." He tightened his grip for a second. "If I'm half the good man I aspire to be, I'd give you back to the Academy so that you can bond with a witch who won't lead you into trouble the way I am. And probably will do again. I seem to be determined to do so."

Aden was too furious to temper his reaction. He bolted upright, pulling away from James. "Don't you dare! I don't want another witch. I belong to you. Only you, and whatever danger you face, I will face with you. If you take me back, I'll only run right back here."

In the dim moonlight showing around the curtains, Aden could make out how James smiled at his outburst. When the man reached for him, Aden half expected a slap, yet didn't care. Loving his witch was more powerful than any other emotion, more important than any risk he took by sticking to the man's side.

Of course James didn't hit him. Aden was beginning to be pretty sure he never would. Cupping the back of his neck, James pulled him back to his side.

"Where's that docile, obedient familiar I brought home only a couple of days ago?" There was humor in James' tone.

Aden settled down against him, this time with James' arm around him. It had to be painful but Aden liked the closeness too much to resist even for the sake of his witch's comfort.

"I'm still here. I'll do anything you tell me to do except leave. I just can't, James. It would kill me to lose you now."

"That feeling would go away once you bond with another witch." James sounded strained.

"You don't want me to do that."

"No, I don't. But it would be best for you."

"I'd fight him. He'd have to force me and even then, I'd hate being bonded with him for the rest of my life. I'm sure of it." He was, too. For reasons that he didn't understand, there was no way bonding with another witch would cause him to lose this feeling of love even as his nature would compel him to obey his new master.

"Seems like we're stuck with each other then."

"Yes." He hesitated before asking the next question. "Are you mad at me?"

James chuckled. "Never, baby. Now go to sleep. We have another big day ahead of us."

This time, Aden dropped off within seconds.

Chapter Eight

Aden was grateful that James had paid the tailor extra money to finish his suit that very morning. It was strange to be dressed like non-familiar men. The clothing hugged his body in a way that his smock didn't. He could understand why familiars were expected to wear something different. Shifting in this outfit would damage the fabric and rip out the stitches. Even his relatively small animal shape would stress the suit as he fought to get free. Such a horrible waste of money. He hoped there would be no need to take the risk of ruining such a lovely gift from his witch.

James appeared unconcerned about that and about everything, really, as he sauntered into the loud, busy room of the newspaper. The men working there didn't give either of them a second glance. Being unremarkable was a new experience for Aden. He liked not having the kind of attention he was used to getting. It had been necessary to get accustomed to stares and glares because that was the life of a familiar. Now, he understood for the first time that his clothing more than anything was what caught people's attention. As James had said, normal humans didn't always perceive what they were. Only witches and other familiars could easily recognize their own.

He followed in James' wake as he crossed the room to a desk in the far corner. A harried-looking man with a shock of bright red hair sat typing two-fingered with a pencil clenched between his teeth. He was concentrating on what he was doing so intently that it took a few seconds for him to notice James standing in front of him with his hands stuck in his pockets.

Finally, he glanced up and sat back in his chair with a broad grin. "Well, well, look what the cat's dragged in. How are you, James?"

James rocked back on his heels. "Fine as a sunny day, Mike." He nodded toward Aden. "Got myself a familiar."

Mike's eyes swung toward Aden. "Pretty. A boy, then? I'm a wee bit surprised."

James gave a rueful grin. "As am I, but Aden is a snow leopard and damned if he isn't the asset I need to get my business going. Say hello to my old friend Michael O'Malley, Aden."

Aden stood still, not sure what to do with his hands, settling on clasping them behind his back. "How do you do, sir."

Mike chuckled. "Polite and pretty." He eyed James again. "I'd offer you a seat but I don't rank any chairs for visitors. If it's a private conversation you're after, we'll need to step outside."

"Exactly what I'm looking for."

James followed Mike and Aden followed James as they wended their way through the room and out of a back door. As soon as they reached a low stone wall,

Mike stopped and took out a pre-rolled cigarette and a box of matches from his pocket. Everyone waited until he lit the smelly thing before getting down to business.

"Got yourself in a spot of trouble again, have you?"

With his hands still in his pockets, James leaned against the wall. "You've heard that, have you?"

Mike blew an impressive smoke ring. "Not as such. I know there was a raid in Freaktown. Very unusual, and orchestrated by someone high up in city government."

"I can't confirm that I was anywhere near that," James said with a smile.

"Of course not. Then there was this gossip floating around this morning that a certain disgraced copper and his leopard familiar crashed a fancy do last night." He grinned at Aden. "Caused quite a stir, it did."

Uneasy with the attention, Aden moved to huddle on James' other side. His witch didn't hesitate to hug him around the waist.

"If one were to speculate, Mike, as to who ordered that raid and who is in bed with Robert Appleton's soon-to-be-widowed wife, what name would come to mind?"

Mike studied his cigarette before answering. "One hears that she and the mayor's secretary are quite close, which sounds weird, but not if you factor in that he's a younger son of a Brahmin family down on its luck. It's also true that man does nothing without the mayor's blessing. He's his sentry and lapdog with ambitions of running for office himself."

"He's also a witch."

The newsman didn't seem surprised by that statement.

He sucked tobacco deep into his lungs before letting it out again. "There's been speculation. And *his* assistant is said to be a familiar. Don't you know?"

"I only met the man last night and there was no one with him. Although someone set a couple of dogs on me last night."

Mike looked him up and down. "You look fine, other than that split lip." He slipped his gaze to Aden. "I suppose your familiar is as protective of you as Wyles' familiar is of him. Be glad he's not the one who came after you." He shuddered theatrically. "One hears it can get very messy. Wolverine," he whispered.

"I can take him, whatever he is." Aden hadn't meant to say anything. It wasn't his place to do so, and he wasn't in a position to make that kind of promise anyway. His need to protect James was a hot ball of fury that he couldn't ignore.

Instead of admonishing him, James turned his head to give him a smile. "Let's hope it doesn't come to a fight, baby."

Mike snorted and snuffed out what was left of his cigarette with his boot heel. "Baby, is it? Fallen hard, have you? What would Father Mark say about that?"

At the mention of the priest's name, Aden stiffened. Had this newspaper man sniffed out where Josie was? Maybe he knew more than he was letting on?

James squeezed him once in reassurance. "We're getting off topic. Do you think the mayor might be worried about certain…information that could be floating about that wouldn't hold him in a flattering light?"

The newsman shook his head. "I wouldn't have thought so. The man has a reputation of being a standup citizen."

"Lots of men hide their true selves from the public."

"Yeah, but my feeling is he's the real deal. Naturally, if some evidence to the contrary were to turn up, my editor would be very keen to publish it. At least I hope so. You wouldn't happen to know of any?"

"Not as yet." Butter wouldn't melt in James' mouth as he stared back at his friend. "It's good to know that there would be some outlet for secrets if they came to light. Then again, if there are any, they wouldn't be mine to give."

"Understood, James. You always were too honest for your own good. Just be careful, heh? Pissing off a state senator and the police commissioner over a bit of fluff is one thing. More powerful men than either of them often have things they want to keep buried that are important enough to kill over."

The words chilled Aden's blood. James gave him another squeeze and a wave of calm overtook him. He relaxed against his witch.

"Understood, Mike. I just needed some confirmation that my repulsion toward someone was based on more substance than my personal feeling. Thanks for the chat."

James and Mike shook hands. The newsman winked at Aden as he followed James away.

They left the building and, having taken the trolley and not James' flashy automobile, they returned to the public transportation. But they didn't go home. Rather, James led Aden to a different route, giving him a view of a part of the city he hadn't seen before. It was a kind of thrill riding the trolley. It tooled along at a fast clip, stopping to let passengers on and off. People were crammed in. James tucked them into the back of the car, holding onto a strap with one hand and Aden's waist with the other. They got a few strange looks but James simply smiled as if he didn't have a care in the world.

They switched over to the underground portion of the transportation system, giving Aden a new, exciting experience of being driven along beneath the street. The darkness of the tunnels didn't bother him. He could imagine himself running through them along the track. In his animal form, he had excellent eyesight. He'd been told his eyes even glowed in the dark. Such a skill might prove very useful in his master's work, although he shuddered to imagine what danger there was in playing cat and mouse with the large trolleys.

His musings came to an end on Tremont Street, where James brought them back above ground. Taking Aden by the arm, he walked into the Boston Common and strolled down the rolling paths through green grass. He stopped where an old woman sold apples out of a basket and bought one for each of them. Taking a bite out of his, he handed Aden the other one, then continued on their way. Aden nibbled at his apple, not wanting to spill any of its juices on his nice new waistcoat and shirt. By the time they crossed Charles Street into the Boston Public Garden, James had chewed through all the flesh. He tossed the apple core into some nearby bushes before taking out his handkerchief and wiping his hands clean.

As he did so, James made a lazy circle, staring all around them. "They're good. I'll give them that. Managed to stick with us all the way."

Aden sucked up some apple juice before it dripped down his hand. "I'm sorry, what are you talking about?"

James swiped his thumb across Aden's chin. "The men who've been tasked with following us. I spotted them first thing this morning when we left the apartment."

Aden froze. "We're being watched? But we went to the newspaper. They'll know that."

"Sure they will, baby. They'd have been surprised if I hadn't. So long as I don't have a book under my arm, there's nothing I can do to hurt anyone. Right now, they're only interested in my leading them to Josie."

With his stomach knotted with sudden tension, Aden's appetite fled. He tossed what was left of his apple as James had done, then licked the sticky residue off his fingers.

James inhaled sharply and his nostrils flared. "Are you trying to get us arrested for indecent exposure, baby?"

Aden blinked at him, confused. Then he realized that James was staring at his mouth. Aden quickly dropped his hand. "Sorry, I didn't mean to tease you. *Did* I tease you?"

It was hard to believe that he could capture James' attention simply by sucking on his fingers. The thought led immediately to memories of being on his knees with James' cock buried as deep as Aden could take it into his mouth. He felt himself harden, which surprised him. Getting aroused without effort was new to him. A quick glance told him James was equally so. He appreciated at that moment the benefit of snug trousers over a loose smock. His dick and balls ached in the confinement but at least his erection wasn't obvious unless one looked for it.

Which James was doing. The look of hunger in the man's eyes was both gratifying and alarming. He had no doubt that if they'd been alone, his witch would have him on his hands and knees in an instant.

Aden swallowed hard in an effort to bring moisture to his dry mouth. "I think, um, I need to sit down."

"Good idea before I drag you behind those bushes and mount you right here."

"James!" Thrilled at the provocative warning, Aden could only follow his master to a nearby bench. He sat primly by James' side even though he had the urge to sit on his lap.

A man sauntered their way but stayed far enough that he could only see, not hear them. Aden wanted to look behind him to see if there was someone else there, as well. Knowing James wouldn't want their followers to get wise to being noticed, Aden sat still.

James sat back with his arms stretched across the back of the bench and crossed his legs. He looked to all the world as a relaxed man enjoying a beautiful day in the park. All around them children ran and played, while women—some nannies, others mothers—pushed prams and kept an eye on their charges.

"If you're wondering, that man over there is one who's been following us. The other is behind and to the left. Don't look, though."

"I won't. They must know you've spotted them."

"Maybe. If they're any good at their job. I don't sense that either of them is a witch."

"That's good, then, isn't it? Witches would be harder to, um, lose? Is that the word?"

James smiled and ruffled Aden's hair. Like himself, James hadn't insisted Aden wear a hat. They'd only blow off during a chase, was his reasoning. Aden was glad of it. He liked the feel of the wind in his hair and in particular the gentle touch of James' hand on his head.

"That's exactly the right word, baby. You're learning fast how to be a detective. Having a witch and familiar trail us would be more effective but they're hard to come by. Muscle men are easier and cheaper to hire. They tend to be not so bright. If they had brains, they'd be doing something else. As long as we don't do anything to shake them, they'll just lazily follow us wherever we go."

"Then what do we do?"

"Oh, nothing much. Go home. I'll fuck you silly. And after a while, we sneak out using my cloaking ability. I know just the perfect time to do it, too."

Aden didn't really hear what James was saying, being stuck on the part about what the man was going to do to him back at the apartment.

Aden coughed delicately. "I don't think you should be saying things like that in public, James. Someone might hear."

James chucked him under the chin as he rose. "No one is that close, baby. And I think you like hearing me tell you how much I want you."

Aden's balls tingled with his growing arousal. He stood awkwardly, barely managing to resist the urge to tug at his inseam. "I do like hearing it, James. I…I want you, too."

James grinned. "I know. Come on, baby." Taking Aden by the arm, he hurried them out of the garden.

* * * *

James wasted no time once they were back home. And it was home now, the first one in many years Aden had known. He felt an immediate sense of safety and welcome the moment he stepped inside. But there was no time for him to savor the moment.

"Take off your clothes, baby. Be quick about it, if you please." There was a strain to the man's voice and his hands shook as he hurried to remove his own clothing.

Aden did as told, carefully taking off his coat and tie, unbuttoning his waistcoat and shirt. He treated each article of clothing like the precious possessions that they were. He tried to hang them up in the closet before tackling his trousers, but James plucked them from his hands and tossed them on the bed. The man was already completely naked, his large, hard cock waving in earnest. Aden couldn't imagine how fast James had moved but he understood the motivation for the speed. Knowing that he had that effect on his witch was intoxicating. He would have loved to take things slowly to appreciate every moment, yet James wasn't in the mood to wait.

He grabbed the jar of petroleum jelly and whisked Aden over to the front window. Pressing him face first against the wall, he lowered his head to nibble at Aden's shoulder. The simple touch along with the ridge rubbing against his buttocks caused him to shiver and moan. He hardly noticed what James was doing before his trousers slid to the floor.

The light outside caught his attention. "James," he pushed past the growing pants escaping his mouth. "I think people can see us from the street."

The witch took Aden's earlobe between his teeth and bit with just enough force to make Aden cry out.

"That's the point, baby. Our friends are stationed on the stoop across the way. Let's give them a show that either disgusts or arouses them. Either way, they'll believe we've got plans for the rest of the afternoon."

James rubbed his dick along one of Aden's ass cheeks and groaned loud and long. His warm breath bathed Aden's neck as he peppered him with kisses. At the same time, he reached up to close the curtains. The sun still shone through the sheer cloth, meaning they might still be visible. Aden didn't know how to feel about being put on display. There was no doubt that James was going to mount him soon. His hole spasmed at the thought and his cock couldn't have been harder. He braced his palms against the wall, waiting for James to breach him.

Except the witch didn't do that. He swung Aden around, holding him by his waist so as to keep him from tripping with his trousers bunched around his ankles. He positioned Aden at the table and bent him over it. Now, Aden clutched at the smooth wooden surface. When a slick finger pushed through the ring of his hole, he couldn't hold back a moan. A second one joined it and James thrust them back and forth, stretching Aden's channel with each pass.

"Sorry, baby, I can't wait."

"I don't want you to," was all Aden managed to say before James entered him with one long thrust.

The burn of the man's cock added a surprising goose to Aden's arousal. His dick jerked in response and it didn't take more than a few passes of James' shaft rubbing Aden's prostate before he bucked out an orgasm. He scratched at the table as his body clenched and shook from the force of his pleasure. James caused him to cry out with a last, intense wave of climax by reaching around and wringing his cock dry. Aden collapsed, panting and limp, but his witch had a strong hold on him, keeping him in place as he continued to drill his ass.

It was as if he came out of a dream, such was the fog clouding James' mind. He slowly regained his senses, although his cock spasmed once again in a desperate effort to pump more cum into his familiar's ass. The possessiveness that washed over him was frightening in its intensity, but the pure joy and satiation radiating from his boy reassured him. They were well and truly bonded with no barriers between them. All doubt about his ability to take care of his familiar fled, leaving only a well of emotion that he thought he had a word for.

No, it's too early.

Later, when they were free of this Appleton mess, he'd have time to explore how he felt about Aden and what their relationship truly meant for him. They had a lifetime to look forward to and with the familiar already declaring his love for him, James could afford to take a more measured approach. He was supposed to be the sensible one, after all.

He chuckled inwardly. He hadn't shown much sense or restraint in the last few minutes. Despite saying that he was putting on a show for the goons keeping tabs on them, the truth was he couldn't have waited to sink into Aden's luscious ass no matter what. Even now, he held the boy by the waist to keep him from tripping over his trousers.

It took a humbling amount of effort, but James lifted Aden into his arms and brought him to the bed. He knelt down to finish the boy's disrobing, then settled him onto the pillow and lay down beside him. They had time for a quick nap. Closing his eyes, he let himself drift off. By the time he opened them again, the sun was beginning to set. The familiar was in the bathroom running the water. James pushed up to get a look at what the boy was doing.

"Are you washing your trousers?" A loud yawn overtook him.

Aden came in holding the piece of clothing up. "Look what happened. Some of my cum dribbled on them." The boy looked close to tears.

James opened his arms with a grin. "Come here, baby. It's okay."

Aden stepped closer but didn't go into his embrace. "They were so dear. I can't believe I let them get dirty."

Realizing that this was serious to the familiar, James dropped his arms and his smile. "I'm sure you got it all out. I've had plenty of practice getting that sort of thing out of my own clothes when I was younger and came in my sleep. I didn't want my mother to know."

Aden scrutinized his trousers. "I think I managed to clean it." He frowned. "Next time, please give me a chance to fully undress. And hang my clothing up properly."

"I will. I promise. Um, you're okay otherwise?" As with before, he'd been pretty rough in his need to find his own pleasure.

Aden's cheeks pinked. "I'm very well. As I'm sure you know. I came almost immediately." His tone was almost accusatory.

"Sorry, baby. Next time, I'll grip your cock so hard, you won't be able to come until I let you. You'd like that, wouldn't you?"

Aden pouted. "Yes, actually."

"Good." Feeling energized, James stood and stretched. He liked how Aden watched him with shy interest. "Let me take those." He plucked the damp trousers from Aden's hands and draped them over a chair. "They'll dry fine overnight. I'm afraid you'll need to wear your smock for what I have planned anyway."

"All right."

"Aren't you going to ask me what the plan is?"

Aden shrugged. "There's no point in taking the time for you to tell me. I trust you know what you're doing. I'll follow you anywhere, James."

The utter devotion he heard in those words and saw in the boy's eyes humbled him. No matter what, he'd do everything in his power to keep him safe.

"Make us some sandwiches, will you? I need to wash up. We don't have much time."

"For what?"

"To be ready to go before Mrs. Santorino leaves with her brood."

With that he went into the bathroom, whistling as he did so.

Chapter Nine

Some things in life could be counted on even if you didn't understand at the time they would be needed. Every weekday evening at six o'clock, Mrs. Santorino gathered her five boisterous children and herded them to the local Catholic church for mass. As they exited the building, they caused a small riot and provided the perfect cover for a cloaked James and Aden to slip through without anyone watching noticing that somehow the door was magically opening or staying that way longer than the people leaving would justify. The two men watching the building gave only a cursory glance at the descending swarm of immaculately cleaned and dressed children and their harried, yet iron-fisted mother.

With his arm tightly around his familiar's waist, James circled around the children and hurried in the opposite direction. He didn't release the cloaking until he'd turned a corner and was sure they weren't being followed. It took a lot of energy to make himself and someone else invisible even for a short time. He allowed himself a minute to lean against a brick wall and catch his breath.

Aden stared at him. "Are you all right?"

James nodded, still a bit breathless. "Not to worry, baby. I just need a moment to recover." He glanced around the corner of the building to make sure they still weren't being followed. "Okay, we're clear."

He took Aden by the arm and steered him down the street. There was a trolley station nearby that would eventually get them to where they needed to go. God, but he wished he could use his automobile. Wyles — if he was indeed the person orchestrating the tailing — would have thought to have that watched, too. His mode of transportation was flashy as well as convenient. He'd have to settle for getting around as he'd always done. Aware that Aden seemed nervous among the crush of passengers, he kept him close. He stared down a few disapproving gawkers. Everyone could tell the boy was a familiar by his clothing, so there was nothing for them to harp on about the way he held Aden tightly against his body. The feel of it reminded him of the passion they'd shared a few hours ago.

And if he allowed himself to focus on those memories, there'd be a whole lot for the other passengers to rightly disapprove of.

James got off short of his destination and scanned the area continuously before heading for the rectory.

"Do you think we're still being followed after all the effort you went to?" Aden stuck close to James' side.

"No, but we can't be too careful. The last thing I want is to lead those assholes right to Josie."

"What are we going to talk to him about, if I may ask?"

"Baby, I've told you to ask me anything, anytime. And, in answer to your question, I need to get the location of the book out of him. I'm running blind here. The mayor is probably pulling the strings behind the scenes, so I have to see what Appleton has on him. It might give me leverage to help Josie."

"I don't know that he trusts us that much, and I can't say I blame him."

"You're probably right, but I have to do my best to convince him."

With one eye still on the lookout for Wyles' goons, James led the way down the path to the rectory. Father Mark would be giving Mass at this time, too. He had to trust Josie would be able to see who was knocking to let them in. The young man didn't disappoint him.

Josie opened the door in his shirt sleeves just enough to let them slip through, then shut it firmly behind them. "You have news?"

James grimaced. "Sort of. Let's go to the room Father Mark gave you to keep this as private as we can."

Josie nodded, obviously dying to ask questions, and went up the back stairs to a small room with one narrow window covered with a thick curtain. There was nowhere to sit other than a cot, so they stood in the middle of the room.

James shoved his hands in his pockets. "I need the book, Josie. It's the only way I'm going to be able to help you." He proceeded to override the boy's objections by filling him in on what had happened since they'd left him.

Josie's mouth formed a thin line as he turned away and paced as much as the confined space would allow. "I'm sorry you got hurt."

"That's not important. It's comes with the job," he added when he could tell that Josie didn't buy that dismissal of the attack. "What matters now is that none of us will be safe until we broker a deal with the right person.

"I believe that to be Wyles because he's the mayor's first line of defense. If we can lay out a deal to the secretary that protects the mayor as well as us, the man will take it to his boss and make it happen. The thing is, I have to know what the mayor is trying to hide to show that I have the goods. Otherwise, why would they bother listening to me at all?"

Josie didn't look convinced.

Aden stepped forward. "James is right, Josie. All those people I saw at the party...they were bathed in fear. I could *smell* it on them. They're so afraid that they'll be found lacking in some way, and ostracized from that stupid society they cling to, that they will do anything, say anything to be safe. James needs the power to benefit from that basic fear in their hearts."

James looked at his familiar with surprise. He'd often thought the same thing about the upper class, given what he'd observed as a copper. Insecurity would have been what he'd have called it, but fear worked just as well.

He turned his attention back to Josie. "Please. Trust me."

With a sigh, Josie threw up his hands. "Like I have a choice. Father Mark has been very kind but the day after tomorrow, I have to be out of here. I want to be able to leave without looking over my shoulder all the time."

James' heartbeat sped up. This was what he'd hoped for. "Where is it? Is the location something I can easily access?"

"From what I've seen, I'm sure you'll have no trouble. It's somewhere no one would think to look because you see, I developed a tendre for a stable boy." He shrugged on a chuckle. "Scandalous, isn't it? He lives above the mews and no respectable Appleton would ever go to such a hovel even for a tumble. Fortunately, I have no such scruples. Look under the floorboard where he keeps his trunk. And be sure he doesn't see you. He has no idea that I've hidden anything there. I don't want him to get trapped between affection for me and loyalty to the household. He needs the job."

James clasped Josie's hand and squeezed. "Perfect. Thank you, and I promise not to betray the trust you've given us."

* * * *

Aden crouched behind the hedge in animal form as he waited for James to return. Cloaking took a lot out of the witch, so it made sense that he'd enter the mews alone. And the horses would get agitated if they scented his leopard, which meant he had to stay well away. James hadn't been gone that long, yet with each passing minute Aden became more concerned. He twitched his tail and sniffed furiously. Finally, he caught his master's scent and in the next instant the man was beside him.

"Let's go." James patted his satchel, a silent answer to Aden's mental question.

He has the book.

It was dark and the streets were relatively empty. Aden padded beside James as they walked to the apartment. The trolley was shut down for the night and without James' automobile, they had no choice but to travel by foot. It was a long, tedious journey, made more so given Aden's curiosity about what they'd learn from Appleton's dirty ledger. When they were within a block of home, James cloaked them. The two men who'd been watching the building had been replaced by others, equally bored and even less attentive.

Nevertheless, James headed for the back of the building. "Fire escape," he said in a low voice before jumping to grab the first ladder. Aden easily bounded up the iron stairs and waited for his witch to finish the climb with only human strength and speed to aid him. All the curtains in the apartments were closed and they were very quiet as they made their ascent. At their apartment's level, James pushed open the window he'd cracked before they'd left hours ago. No surprise there, the man thought ahead. Aden shifted into his human skin and reached for his union suit while James shut them in.

James gave him a cocky grin. "What'cha doing, baby?"

Aden blinked a few times. "Getting dressed? Do you want me to put on the smock? Are we going out again?"

James grabbed the union suit and tossed it over a chair. "I like you just as you are. And no, we're going nowhere else." The witch shucked off the satchel, his coat and waistcoat, then toed off his boots before lying against the headboard of the bed. He patted a spot next to him. "Come here. We can read the book together."

Aden's face heated up but he did as told, snuggling against James' side. His dick reacted to the proximity with alarming speed. "Sorry." He tried to move away so that his erection wouldn't poke his witch's side.

James curled a hand around Aden's arm and pulled him back. "I'm not." He frowned as he opened the Appleton ledger. "Sadly, I probably can't do anything to ease your discomfort any time soon. This thing is not in alphabetical order. I'll have to read every page to find anything useful."

Resting his head against James' shoulder, Aden peered at the pages as the man slowly turned each page. "There are so many names and not a lot of detail about what Mr. Appleton has on each person."

James hummed. "Some of this doesn't require a lot of detail. Look at this. *Senator Gilmore, adultery.* Then there are five women's names, some with dates. I guess that sums it up nicely. The good senator doesn't want his constituents to know he plays away while undoubtedly showing off his wife and children on the campaign trail."

"I thought wealthy, powerful men were expected to have mistresses."

"Indeed they are, baby. Such men can get away with whatever they want compared to the average man, but it's not supposed to be out in the open. And Gilmore might portray himself as particularly pious. In any event, look at these numbers listed under his name. I'm betting these are dollars and dates."

Aden's eyes popped at how many zeros were next to the money figures. It seemed inconceivable that one man could possess so much that he could afford to pay huge amounts for blackmail. He snuggled closer to James, enjoying the scent of the man — the earthy smell of sweat from their walk with a hint of the bergamot aftershave he'd put on that morning. His cock twitched and he couldn't resist rubbing it against his master's hip.

James chuckled and reached between them to clasp the shaft even as he continued to turn pages. The warm hold, delivered with just a bit of pressure, caused Aden to moan despite his efforts to bite it back. When James scraped his thumbnail through the slit of Aden's cock, it caused him to jerk and gasp.

He swallowed hard. "If you keep that up, I'm going to come in your hand." He gritted his teeth as his balls tightened.

"Uh, uh. I don't think so."

James' grip choked off the burgeoning orgasm at the root of Aden's dick. He stuttered out with both frustration and relief. He really didn't want to distract either of them with his unbridled and untimely need. At the same time, he was already desperate to find his release. After a few seconds, James continued stroking him. Each time Aden could feel himself about to come, the witch put a vice grip on his cock. It seemed like an eternity where the only sounds in the room were of pages being turned and Aden's harsh breaths and pathetic whimpers.

Finally, he could stand no more. "Please." His voice was a strained whisper.

Saying nothing and with his eyes fixed on the page in front of him, James began to jerk Aden's dick in earnest. It took nothing to make him climax. This time, his witch didn't try to stop him. Instead, he stroked every last drop of cum out. Aden collapsed against the man, spent and suddenly exhausted. He could barely keep his eyes open. But his master wasn't done with him yet.

Wiggling his sticky fingers in front of him, James said, "Lick."

It took Aden a moment to understand what he was being told to do. He wasn't sure he liked the idea of tasting his own cum. He had been the one to lack control, though, so it was only fair that he clean up the mess. Licking that hand clean would be easier than getting up and wetting a cloth. He just wanted to sleep, despite also wanting to read the book along with James.

Aden opened his mouth a little and stuck out his tongue. He flicked it against one finger. Salty bitterness, not unlike what he'd tasted from his master during the blow job, slid along his taste buds. It wasn't bad. He could do it...and enjoy it. Grabbing James' hand, he turned it to lap at the man's palm, then sucked on each finger. He pretended that each one was a small dick and gave them the best blow job he could.

James groaned and tugged his hand free. "Now you have me all worked up, baby. Too bad I've a job to do. As soon as I find what I'm looking for, I promise I'll drill you into the mattress."

Pleased at the effect he had on his witch, Aden settled down again, a smile on his face. He couldn't hold back the yawn, however, and his eyelids simply would not stay open.

* * * *

Aden woke with a start. James had sat up and was staring intently at a page. "Did you find it?" He pushed up and carded hair away from his face. "Is there something about the mayor?"

James shook his head. "I found what I needed, but it's not about the mayor."

Aden followed the man's finger and saw what he was reading. He gasped. "It's Wyles!"

"Yes, indeed. The very proper private secretary likes to gamble. And apparently he cheats."

"Cheats how?"

"It doesn't say, but the amounts he's paid are smaller than many of the others. I don't suppose a man in his position makes nearly as much money as these other victims. It can't be that Wyles is acting as a go-between for the mayor. That man comes from *money*. Appleton was shrewd enough to keep Wyles to payments he could afford. For now. Who knows how high Wyles will climb in the world. This blackmail scheme acts like an annuity—a well you can dip into over and over again so long as you possess this information."

"Like Mrs. Appleton."

"Yes, she certainly intends to pick up where her almost-dead husband left off."

James abruptly shut the book, put it on his nightstand and rose to undress. "And I bet Wyles does, too. They've come together in an unholy alliance. She's latched onto a man who can successfully continue with the blackmail for her and he gets to keep his own secret hidden while also learning about others to exploit them.

"I have no idea how long Appleton has to live, but once they have this book, his demise will be hurried up." The man stripped off his union suit to expose his erect cock.

Aden's brain got scrambled by the sight. "You think they'll kill him?" he managed to say as his witch stalked toward the bed with the kind of hungry grace worthy of his own spirit animal.

"Oh yes. The old pillow over the face should do it."

James palmed his cock with one hand while rummaging for the petroleum jelly with the other. He slicked up his dick, then climbed back onto the bed. He had Aden sprawled on his back with his legs spread wide in a blink of an eye. James wedged his body between Aden's legs and, using one hand on the back of his knee, lifted one leg to settle himself flush against Aden's groin.

Aden breathed hard, bracing for the invasion. He gripped the bedcovers, but kept his eyes open and on his witch. "They'll kill Josie, too, won't they?"

"Not if I can help it. Sorry, baby, can't go slowly this time."

"I don't want you to." He forced his sphincter to relax and still he cried out at the sudden stretch and burn of James' cock as it thrust into him to the hilt.

James grunted and went still, giving Aden a chance to accommodate him. "We'll stop them. The key is Wyles. Melinda could lose her money but she'll move onto another meal-ticket. Wyles could end up completely ruined. Christ, Jesus, you're tight."

Seeing the strain on James' face as he tried to rein in his thrusts, Aden bucked up to encourage him. "Fuck me, James. As hard and fast as you want."

The witch needed no further invitation. He pulled back so that the tip of his cock was just inside Aden's passage, then thrust in again. He set up a furious pace, surging back and forth with long, hard strokes. With each roll of his hips, the man sent sparks of pleasure through Aden. The sound of their flesh smacking together mingled with their harsh breaths and deep moans. Aden tried to set a rhythm of his own to meet the thrust and drive the dick further into his ass.

How did this happen? A few short days ago, he'd been a shy virgin. Now, he demanded to be fucked like a wanton whore. Or lover. That was how he thought of them, the love he felt and the affection he knew James held for him making this sweeter. He didn't want to take any cock, only his witch's.

When James cried out and warm cum coated Aden's insides, he let himself go. He didn't need anyone's hand on his shaft. The stroking of his prostate was all that he needed. The weight of James' body as the man collapsed pressed him into the mattress. He let go of the covers and hugged James tightly to him.

"What are we going to do next?" he asked as his mind and breath returned to him.

James lifted up on his arms to capture Aden's mouth in a soft kiss. "We're going to pay Wyles a visit at his office. In the morning, I'm going to give his goons a message that I want to meet him at City Hall after hours and make a deal about the book. He'll believe me because he thinks everyone has a price to violate their principles."

Aden dared to press his face up to kiss James back. It lacked skill, he knew, but hoped his witch saw the emotion behind it. "He might set a trap for us."

James chuckled. "God, you're beautiful and smart with it. He will most definitely try to set some kind of trap. I promise, though, to keep you safe."

"I know you will, James." What he really meant was that he was going to keep his witch safe, too. He'd rip

Wyles' throat out before he let anything happen to the man he loved.

* * * *

James whistled his way across the street, unable to keep from taking jaunty steps and grinning broadly. It was a beautiful morning, the kind that would put even the most taciturn of people in a good mood. But that wasn't what gave him such a lift. No, it was the sure knowledge that Aden slept deeply and peacefully in the bed they now shared after a long night of investigation and bonding. He didn't have to worry that he'd been overly enthusiastic or overbearing with his familiar. He could *feel* the boy's deep satisfaction in what they'd shared. The bond between them had grown exponentially stronger. His witch power surged within him. A good thing, too, given the heavy task he faced later that day.

It was more than merely his enhanced talent, though, that put the spring in his step and made him more confident in his job. The emotional closeness he'd forged with his familiar was on a purely human level. His feelings for the boy had sprung up and nearly overwhelmed him. Far from being disturbing, he was beginning to find that his newly developed attachment to another *man*, of all things, filled in a piece of him that had been missing. Something he'd been looking for without even realizing it. His whole life, he'd been told by words and deeds that men found a suitable wife, whom they had to at least tolerate, and produce a family. Love was a luxury most people couldn't afford, but he might be lucky enough for that emotion to form over time. He hadn't given it much thought, truth be told. He'd been married to his job and had seen how such dedication wasn't fair to a wife. Then he'd been focused on developing his seeker skills to make a living. He'd expected a familiar to help him. He hadn't considered the possibility that one would create for him that kind of family bond that others took for granted.

Until now.

Aden was changing everything James had assumed about his life. Far from being annoyed at having to make room for someone else, he looked forward to returning to his small apartment and sliding into bed with his familiar. Not because he craved even more sex, although his cock certainly stirred at the mere thought of it. He only wanted to hug the boy close to him, inhale his unique scent and bask in the simple peace of having Aden to himself. And to know the boy was safe in his embrace. Whatever else he felt for his familiar, he knew it was his duty and his honor to keep him from harm.

That thought steeled his spine as he approached the two men loitering across from his building, trying to look as if they weren't watching him. And failing. On top of everything else, Wyles seemed to be a cheapskate. His hired thugs were third rate at best.

James widened his grin. "Good morning, boys. I have something for you."

When he reached into the pocket of his waistcoat, the men straightened and hovered their hands by their trouser pockets. *Morons.* As if James could hide a gun in such a small space. He whipped out the piece of paper and held it in front of them.

"I have a letter for Mr. Wyles, if you please."

The older of the two sneered. "Don't know who you mean. We're not your errand boys."

James waved the letter. "Now, now. Your master isn't going to appreciate it if you put me off. This is a message for him about meeting this evening. I have a proposition for him that will benefit us all. He'll understand," he added when they still hesitated to take the paper.

Finally, the older man snatched the letter from James' hand. "Don't know what you're going on about but it might be I know a fella who knows this Mr. Wyles." He took a step toward James. "Why don't we go and see him together? No sense in wasting a trip with all this foolishness." The man flapped the paper.

James shook his head. "We're doing this on my terms or not at all. Your master will just have to accept that there are some things he can't control, but if he's smart, we both walk away from a meeting tonight happy fellows."

James didn't bother to wait for a reply. He turned on his heel and walked back to his apartment building without glancing over his shoulder. There was no doubt in his mind that the hired goons would deliver the message. And he was certain, as well, that Wyles would be ready to receive him in his office after hours. Whether they came to a deal or not remained to be seen. They were running out of time, however, so a bold move had to be taken. He'd been careful to work in his knowledge of Wyles' weakness into the wording of his invitation so that there would be no doubt he at least had access to the information in the Appleton ledger.

The trick was going to be securing the book in order for the meeting to be meaningful. He had formed a plan for that, of course. He couldn't afford to risk bringing it with him and the moment he and Aden left, Wyles' men were sure to break into his apartment to search for it. His cloaking ability could be used to hide it for a while, but that took more energy than he was willing to devote to protecting the book when he might need to use it to shield himself and Aden. His decision of where to hide it didn't sit well with him. Too bad he didn't have a better one.

James was quiet as he reentered the apartment so as to not wake Aden. The familiar was where he'd left him, curled up on his side under the bed covers. The peaceful expression on the boy's beautiful face caused James to freeze and simply…stare. His heart did a slow roll and his breath stuttered out of him.

Whatever resolve he'd had to not fall in love with his familiar evaporated in that moment. He was utterly taken by the intensity of the feeling. And while his dick rallied at the sight of a ready and willing boy for the taking, this had nothing to do with carnal desire. That was a bonus, as was the boost in his power. The core of what he wanted from Aden, with Aden, was far more typically human. A mere day ago, he'd shied away from the emotion. Now, he wondered what he'd been worried about. It was wonderful.

Even though James made no sound, Aden stirred and woke with wide eyes. They stared at each other for a few seconds before the familiar held out his hand.

"I'm glad to see you again, too, James. Come back to bed."

James tore off his clothes and gathered the boy in his arms. "You're mine."

"Yes," was Aden's simple reply before he dropped back into sleep.

Chapter Ten

James glanced at Aden while maneuvering around a wagon. The familiar was worried, he could tell. Not that he'd questioned James' plan on where to hide the ledger. He was too well trained to be obedient to do so. But the boy's expression, visible even past the large goggles he wore, made his thoughts on the matter clear. As did the way he clutched at the satchel that contained the book.

"It'll be fine. You'll see. Kitty is smart and brave. She'll understand and no one would dare break into the Sisters' house even if they thought it was the hiding place."

Aden's only response was to nod once and hug the satchel more tightly to him. James understood. Not only was the familiar obviously agitated about what was to come that night, but the travel noise from the engine, the wind, and the street around them made speaking difficult. As much as James loved his automobile, he couldn't help hoping that the makers of this astounding invention would soon find a way to enclose it. The goggles were both dashing and annoying and the wind in his face was both exhilarating and…well, annoying. Plus, he wanted to be able to talk to his familiar. He liked doing so, and although they could speak telepathically, it took energy, as everything else he did as witch. He couldn't afford to strike up a conversation in their minds as if it were a lazy Sunday, instead of a night where he might have to call on all of his witch ability to come through unscathed.

He pulled up in front of the Back Bay mansion and shut off the engine. "Let's go around back. We might not be servants, but I can't quite think of us as guests, either."

"That sounds like a good idea. I'm not comfortable going through the front door, either."

James hurried around to the passenger side to liberate the heavy satchel from the boy and help him out. Maybe his hands lingered a little too long on Aden's waist and his gaze homed immediately onto the boy's lips. There were too many people nearby for him to give in to the impulse to kiss him, so he settled for clutching one hand and leading him around to the kitchen door.

It was Kitty who opened the door even before the knock.

"Saints preserve us, James. We could hear that loud machine of yours through the front parlor windows." She stepped aside to give them room to enter into a kitchen that smelled of roasted chicken and freshly baked bread. "Why didn't you come in the front? The Sisters and I are having tea and they hoped you'd join us."

James bussed his sister on the cheek. "A lovely offer and please thank them for us, but we can't stay long." He paused and added in a low voice, "I need to talk to you."

Kitty was no fool. She pursed her lips and narrowed her gaze. "Do you, now? I suppose you should come up to my room."

James gave a firm nod, then let go of Aden's hand. "Wait here. I won't be long."

The cook bustled up, wiping her hands on her apron. "Come on, dear boy. Have a seat and I'll give you a slice of cake and a glass of milk. Not much to you, is there?" She sniffed. "We'll fatten you up, never fear."

Leaving a somewhat bewildered Aden in the kitchen, James hurried up the back stairs in Kitty's wake. Instead of continuing to the upper floor where the servants slept, she turned into the corridor for the floor with the family's bedrooms. She entered the first one on the left, a pretty space with white eyelet bedcovers and curtains and an antique writing desk already piled high with thick books.

His sister shut the door and put her fists on her hips. "What's up, James?"

"I need a favor." He unfastened the clasps of his satchel and pulled out the ledger. "Could you please keep this for me?"

She eyed it suspiciously. "Is that a book of dirty secrets?" She was too clever by half.

"You don't want to know. *I* don't want you to know, but it wasn't my choice to learn. It's safer for you to stay in relative ignorance."

"Safer? And yet you want me to hide it here where the Sisters and I live, not to mention the servants."

"No one has any reason to know that, nor would they be so bold as to break into the house of such wealthy and influential women unless they were sure of it being worth the risk. Trust me. If I thought otherwise, I wouldn't ask."

Kitty puffed out a breath. "Oh, very well." She took the ledger and tucked it into the bottom of the stack of books on her desk. "Hiding in plain sight makes the most sense to me."

She was right. With everything there being bound by leather and looking worn, it didn't stand out. That was assuming that anyone would ever venture into this particular room to search for the damn thing.

James went over to her and put his hand on her arm. "Thank you. I promise this will all be over after tonight. I'll come fetch it in the morning. If anyone else does, even if it's the police, pretend you have no idea what they are talking about."

Kitty opened her eyes and fluttered her lashes. "Why I'm just a poor, ignorant girl from Southie. What do I know about anything?"

James laughed. "Well, you've convinced me." He reached for a book on the top of the pile. "Mind if I borrow this?" At her unspoken question, he explained. "Anyone watching me will see that my satchel is as full as it was when I left my apartment."

"Very clever. I do hope you know what you are doing, James."

"I think so. It's risky but I don't know any other way to extricate myself and Aden from this mess. Plus, I'm not going to cave to the pressure of throwing Josie Appleton to the wolves. I couldn't live with myself if I did."

"You've always been the best of us, Seamus Byrne."
She kissed his cheek. "Do take care with your Aden.
He's such a nice boy. I really like him."

James couldn't keep the grin off his face. "I really
like him, too. Maybe I shouldn't so much…"

"Who's to say you shouldn't? You've always cut
your own path. Don't stop now."

"Hand to God, I won't."

* * * *

James shoved Aden behind him the moment one of
Wyles' men approached them outside the apartment.

The men curled his lip as he switched his gaze
between Aden and James. "Don't get yourself
exercised, boyo. I'm here to deliver a message back."

"I didn't expect a response. My letter was quite clear
on that. Mr. Wyles knows I intend to show up no matter
what."

The man shrugged. "Like I care. You're getting one
anyway. Come in the side door so as not to attract too
much attention. His assistant, Mr. Pavel, will be there
to let you in and show you the way." His gaze flicked
to Aden. "He said to keep your…*familiar* away. He
won't abide having that animal in his office."

James leaned toward the man. "I will if he will."

The man backed up. "Don't know what you mean
by that, but then I'm not paid to. I gave you the
message."

With that, the thug hurried back across the street.

James watched until he was sure there was no
physical threat before escorting Aden back inside. He
made sure to bolt the door, then tossed the satchel on

the bed. Its heavy weight caused the mattress to depress.

Aden cocked his head. "Did your sister refuse to hide the ledger?"

As he stripped off his coat, James nodded toward the sack. "Open it."

Aden hesitated for a second before doing so. He pulled out the substitute book and frowned. "Human anatomy?"

James jutted his chin toward the front window. "Those morons outside will be able to confirm, should anyone ask, that my satchel was no more empty when I returned than it was when I left."

Aden tucked the book back into the pack. "That was clever of you."

"I hope so." He went to pull Aden in for a kiss. "Hmm, I taste sugar."

"The cook insisted about the cake. It was very good." His eyes widened. "I should have asked for a slice for you."

"Not to worry, baby." He patted his stomach that was still flat but only because he worked on keeping it that way. "My days of eating cake in the middle of the day are over. But I promise you that when this whole thing is over, I'll take you to tea at one of the fancy hotels. They have lots of sweets."

"You don't have to spend money on me. I'm already eating better than I did at the Academy."

The mere mention of that bleak place, where Aden had spent the last years of his childhood, made James mad and sad. Even though it had been where he'd acquired his familiar, he still wished the boy's life had been better.

"I like pampering you. It makes me happy," he emphasized when it looked as if Aden were going to insist otherwise. "Come on. Being this close to the bed gives me bad ideas. We need to go over the plan for tonight. I don't want Wyles to be in a position to dictate how this meeting is going to go."

He clasped Aden by the waist and brought him over to sit at one end of their small table, while he sat in the other chair. What he really wanted was Aden on his lap but that would be too distracting.

Aden clasped his hands in front of him. "I don't mind if you need to, um, strengthen the bond. You know, before we go out." He dropped his gaze.

"Oh, baby, our bond is plenty strong enough. If I were to fuck you right now, it would be purely for the pleasure of it."

The familiar's cheeks pinked. "I wouldn't mind that, either. I, um, like it. A lot."

"Good because I intend to do it…a lot. Now, back to business." James looked away from the temptation that Aden was and started to lay out his plan.

* * * *

James waited for Wyles' assistant to open the side door of City Hall. It was an impressive building, done in the French Second Empire style, whatever the hell that meant. It was certainly ornate, with three stories on each side and a middle section that went two more floors up. He had no idea where Wyles' office was located. Near the mayor, he assumed, although he didn't know if that would mean fewer people or more being about. He'd watched people stream out of it an hour before, so he didn't think many other than guards were about. He'd picked this time for that very reason.

He patted his coat pocket for the thousandth time to make sure his gun was where he'd put it. The knife slid into the side of his boot was easily felt if he twitched his ankle. He was going into this meeting with as much protection as he had, and that included the leopard sitting by his feet. Sweet Aden showed no signs of worry other than his flicking tail. He'd really wanted to keep the boy at home, but that would have put him at a disadvantage, and probably would have put Aden at greater risk. He had no doubt that his apartment was being tossed at that very moment in a pointless effort to find the ledger.

The door opened suddenly and a dark-haired man with a white streak running down one side stuck his head out. He glared at James, then Aden.

"The beast stays outside. You were told not to bring him."

"I don't answer to Wyles. Nevertheless, I agree to keep my familiar out here. Unlike some other witches, I don't need his proximity to take advantage of his power."

His dismissive tone and veiled insult were not lost on the man. Still, he stepped aside in silent invitation without saying anything more.

"Don't move, Aden. I'll be cross if you do." He patted the leopard on the head before entering the gloom of the building.

He followed whom he assumed was Pavel up two flights of stairs and down a corridor. He spotted what he was looking for and stopped. "Hold up. I need the facilities."

James didn't wait for a response, he slipped inside the lavatory and crossed to the transom window on the far side. He opened it with the pole left for that purpose and hoped there was enough room for Aden to slip in. As there was nothing he could do short of smashing the thing entirely, he was forced to leave it to the boy's cleverness to get inside. He was careful not to shut the outer door completely when he went back into the corridor.

He bared his teeth at Pavel. "I must be nervous about my meeting with the big man."

Making no response, the assistant led him down to the far end of the corridor and knocked once on a door to the right. There was a muffled response that caused the man to open it for James. Once again, he stepped to the side, but he entered right behind him and shut the door.

James ignored the lackey and concentrated on his quarry. He flicked his gaze around the room. "Nice, Wyles. Maybe I should have studied to become a secretary. It certainly comes with lots of perks." James wandered over to a shelf that contained cut-crystal decanters of dark liquids, along with matching crystal glasses. "Mind if I help myself?"

Wyles rose from behind his large, dark-wood desk that was filled with a lot of paper that was intended to convey just how busy he was. He stuck his hands in his pockets.

"Go ahead. I know how you Irish love your whiskey."

Ignoring the sad attempt at an insult, James poured a couple of fingers and took a sip as he held Wyle's gaze. "Very fine, indeed." He stuck his free hand in his pocket and adopted Wyles' relaxed stance. He let time tick by without saying another word.

Wyles finally blinked first. "Well?"

"Well, what?"

"Your letter said you had a proposition to offer."

"Ah, yes. And so I do." He jutted his chin toward Pavel, who remained by the door. "Are you sure you want your…familiar to hear what I have to say?"

Wyles looked only slightly surprised. "It can be easy to hide ourselves from humans, or at least keep them guessing. But a witch knows a witch." He shrugged. "The rumors of my nature aren't very quiet around town. I keep a low profile, though. Unlike you, I've never used my powers to advance my career." His expression made it seem most distasteful to do so.

James took another sip, only to give himself something to do as he sought out Aden in his mind. He could see the great cat slipping easily past the open window, bounding across the lavatory and out of the door. He'd been told to keep to the shadows and only make himself known if James needed him to. Still, he worried that Aden might be bold in his efforts to help. He did appear to worry about James. Possibly as much as he worried about his familiar.

"I've seen the ledger." He was careful not to say he had it. "I know you're in it, Wyles. Not the mayor, as I'd thought at first. You like to gamble."

Wyles shrugged. "So what?"

"And you cheat. That's what. Someone with your political ambitions wouldn't want that to come to light."

Wyles chuckled, almost convincingly. "A minor sin. No one would care and I told Appleton as much. I didn't give him a penny."

James put his glass down. "The ledger says otherwise."

"A lie."

"That makes no sense. No one other than the blackmailer himself would look, so why bother to falsify his records?"

Wyles merely shrugged again.

"Well, in any event, I'm prepared to make a deal. You give up on finding Josiah Appleton. Mrs. Appleton stakes him enough money to go west and start a new life. And you both leave him the fuck alone."

"Assuming I care, what do I get in exchange. The book?"

James forced a chuckle. "No. I don't think I trust you or Mrs. Appleton to stick with the deal. I expect you two intend to pick up where Appleton left off." He could see in the man's expression that he'd hit the mark. "Once Josie is away, we pick a reliable neutral party, someone not in the book, to destroy it in front of both of us. How's that sound?"

Wyles came around his desk and sat on the front edge of it. "Ridiculous. And I don't have to cut a deal with you at all. Right now, my men are pulling up every board and breaking through every wall in your pathetic apartment. I'm sure you have it and soon so will I. Hopefully, your familiar won't get in the way."

Even knowing that Aden wasn't there to be hurt, James' protective instincts reared up. The smug expression on Wyles' face begged to be punched off.

Before he could respond, Pavel stepped forward. "His familiar isn't there, sir. He brought him here. But he's stayed outside."

Wyles straightened to his feet. "You idiot! He's a fucking cat and will have found a way inside. Find him. *Kill* him."

Pavel jumped to open the door and shredded his fine suit as he shifted into a wolverine.

Even though James had been prepared for that animal, the sight of it still chilled his blood. Wolverines were small but known to be so vicious they could defeat larger opponents.

"Pavel is after you in wolverine form. Take care, baby. Hide, don't engage with him."

"I'm fine and ready. I'll lead him away so that he can't hurt you."

"Threatening my familiar was a mistake, asshole. My offer is off the table." James had barely pulled his gun from his pocket when it flew out of his hand with an unseen force that wrenched his wrist.

"A telekinetic. I should have known." He dodged a brass clock that flew his way, smashing against the wall. "Let me show you what a seeker witch can do."

With that, he cloaked.

* * * *

Aden slunk around a corner and crouched. The wolverine was a noisy beast, its claws clacking against the stone flooring as it scampered down the corridor in search of him. He knew that he had the size advantage, but wolverines were known for their aggressive nature that served them well no matter the size of their opponent. Aden couldn't afford to be overly confident in his ability to overcome Pavel, especially as his witch was counting on him for protection. Not that he doubted James' ability to best Wyles. It was simply that the sounds of that fight were ringing in his head and each time he saw objects flying and crashing around through his witch's eyes, he experienced a bone-deep fear that threatened to overwhelm him.

He forced himself to shut off the connection with James. It did the guy no good to be distracted by Aden's emotions. They both needed to focus on their respective foes. Once Aden had dealt with Pavel, he could hurry to James' side to help subdue the telekinetic. Although he couldn't imagine what the plan was now that negotiations had failed so miserably. James had expected this eventuality. It was the very reason why Aden had slipped into the building, yet a full-on battle was so stupid in such a public place that Aden's presence had been out of an abundance of caution.

Knowing that one of his strengths was his agility, Aden decided to lead the wolverine up to tight places requiring balance that would put the familiar at a disadvantage. It would also take them farther away from where the witches battled. As much as he wanted to be by James' side, it was more important that the wolverine kept his focus on Aden and not return to his master. The telekinetic couldn't see James while he was cloaked, but Aden had to assume that the wolverine would smell him. The presence of the beast in the witches' fight would give their enemy a huge advantage that couldn't be borne. So, he peeked around the corner enough for the wolverine to see him, then raced off down the corridor and up the stairs. It was nothing for him to bound up to the next level. The wolverine was fast and a good climber so the distance between them was closing quickly. Aden had no choice but to take the fight as high up as he could, rely on his cat's ability to balance and hope the wolverine couldn't match him. If he could launch an attack from above the creature, he stood a better chance of prevailing.

He only hoped that James' power would also triumph over Wyles'.

* * * *

James struggled to keep his breathing even as he dodged the scattershot assault by Wyles. The witch didn't seem to care that he was destroying his office in his quest to hit James with something to force him to reappear. The sounds of the crashes were loud. It surprised him that no one was coming to investigate. There were guards, surely, even for form's sake, at night. Were they too far away to hear? Asleep? Or, more likely, Wyles had used the clout of the mayor's office to make sure whoever was around would be deaf to anything happening until he told them otherwise.

A paperweight whizzed by his head, too close for comfort. He moved in closer to Wyles in the hopes that the man would expect him to be farther away.

"How long can you keep this up, Byrne? Because I'm not even breaking a sweat here. There's nowhere for you to run."

James was well aware of how true that was. If he opened the door, he would give away his position and Wyles could force the door shut again before James could get through it. The man's power was strong, yet not as strong as James would have expected. Wyles had been bonded with his familiar longer than James had, that was for sure. On some clinical level, it was interesting to have it confirmed that time could make his connection with Aden stronger. Boost his power beyond what already felt like heady heights. At the same time, he could see that there was a limit, or perhaps it was something about Wyles and Pavel's bond that was a bit defective. Although it was impossible to detect what was in the man's heart and mind, he didn't seem concerned about their familiars fighting to the death. Whereas James couldn't bear the thought of Aden being hurt in the slightest.

The mere thought of the boy sent him into a new level of fear. Where was he now? How was he doing against the wolverine? He didn't dare try to reach out to see through the familiar's eyes or distract him with questions. Whatever James was going through at that moment, he was a trained fighter. Aden was a sweet boy who had only gone against a human a day ago. Waging a battle—likely to the death—was not something Aden had been prepared to do. James wasn't sure the boy had it in him, frankly. He should never have brought him. The situation wasn't supposed to have turned to shit so quickly and disastrously. *I should have insisted he return to the Academy.*

Wyles was crazy to react this way. Or perhaps simply desperate. And desperate men were the most dangerous of them all.

To give himself a break from the drain of cloaking, James dropped the protection for a moment. "Is your secret worth all of this, Wyles?" He spread his arms even as he avoided yet another book flying toward his face. He bit back a grunt as it clipped his shoulder. "What's your end game, killing me? You'll find that hard to do and harder to explain."

In answer to the goading, Wyles raised his hand with James' gun in his grasp. "Killing someone who attacked me in my own office? I don't think anyone will question it."

James straightened as the man pointed the gun at him and pulled the trigger.

Chapter Eleven

James rather enjoyed the look of shock and frustration as all that happened when Wyles pulled the trigger was a resounding click. Grimacing, Wyles tried again and got the same results.

"You didn't think I brought a loaded gun with me, did you? I'm never so cavalier about giving an enemy access to my gun. It can always be turned against you if you're not vigilant." He'd learned the hard way from watching another copper get killed by his own weapon wrested away from him.

The bullets weighed heavily in his trousers pocket, but he resisted the temptation to show any indication that they were on his person. This battle wasn't going to be won with a firefight. Wyles curled his lip as he pulled the trigger the third time and even though he got nothing from it, he still kept the gun trained on James. A bead of sweat trickled down the man's temple.

Never one to give up, James offered to talk once more. "Let's settle this little witch bitch down, shall we?

I don't give a rat's ass about your gambling. How do you use your power to cheat, by the way?" He shrugged, buying for time now that he saw his opponent's weakness. He didn't dare focus on Aden for fear of distracting the boy, yet he felt the familiar's confidence in his own fight.

Wyles sent the gun flying toward James. It was easily dodged, so he didn't bother cloaking again. He needed to conserve his energy.

"My sin is not as bad as others laid out in Appleton's book, I'll wager." The man flashed a smile. "So to speak. I merely use my ability to move balls and dice to my winning advantage in roulette and craps. I don't know how Appleton figured it out, but I believe he had spies everywhere and one of them must have been a witch who perceived my power. It doesn't matter. Once I have the book, I'll have no need to earn extra money that way."

James leaned forward. "I couldn't care less what you do with the information. I only want to use the book as currency to protect Josie, as well as myself and my familiar."

Wyles shook his head slowly. "I'm not going to let scum like you and that pervert son of Appleton's walk around freely with my secrets. There's no deal to be had."

With that final statement, chaos was released.

* * * *

Aden kept to the shadows, slinking along the banister and keeping his eyes peeled for the wolverine. That familiar had the same keen eyesight so Aden didn't assume he could hide. His scent alone would lead his enemy to him. His plan was to draw Pavel away from their witches. He knew James was fighting for his life yet didn't dare try to communicate. They both needed to stay focused on their respective battles. And if the unthinkable happened and he could no longer protect his witch, he wanted the wolverine as far from that office as possible to give James a chance to flee.

When he caught sight of the wolverine coming around the corner, he crouched and leapt over the inside courtyard to the next floor. He nearly took a tumble before gaining purchase on the smooth upper railing. He scrambled to balance on the sleek wood, his tail twitching with a combination of fear and excitement. No one had ever taught him how to fight. He still knew how. The instinct was front and center in his animal form. His human heart yearned to save his master from the wolverine's viciousness. Skin was no match for fangs and claws. His own hide wasn't impregnable, but it sure was tougher. And as much as wolverines were known to be formidable foes, he had his love for James to give him extra strength and determination.

He wondered if Pavel had the same incentive.

Aden shut down all thought as the wolverine came bounding into view, clearly spoiling to start the fight. Aden gave the familiar what he wanted.

With a hiss, he struck, jumping onto the wolverine's back and sinking every sharp part of him into the thick fur. The familiar growled and immediately rolled to shake Aden off his back. Expecting the maneuver, Aden twisted to land lightly on his paws and launched into a frontal attack without skipping a beat. His body slammed into the wolverine's and now it was his turn to be pricked by claws. He responded in kind, snarling and snapping his jaws in an effort to latch onto something. He tried to use his larger size to dominate the smaller animal.

The wolverine showed no fear, swiping at Aden's front, before retreating a safe distance. They stood staring at one another, panting, circling, looking for an opening. Aden let Pavel make the next move, then swiped with his longer limb before the other familiar reached him. Blood spurted from the wolverine's face right before he barreled into Aden, sending them both flying in a ball of fury.

* * * *

James had no choice but to cloak once more as a whirlwind of objects flew around the room. Wyles was acting out of control, his eyes gleaming as he waved his arms to guide his ordinary weapons. The familiars were engaged in a pitched battle. The waves of the emotions and energy being expended by Aden washed over James. Instead of cowing him with worry, he became reenergized and more determined to bring Wyles down. There was going to be no deal with the man, no rational outcome of this whole mess. There would be blood—his or Wyles', Aden's or Pavel's. He could do nothing for Aden so long as he was forced to defend himself.

It was time to attack.

It was easy to slip behind the desk by keeping low to the ground. Wyles was trying to hit a standing man, so James crouched and crawled until he was right beside his opponent. He reached into his boot and slid the blade out. Then he stood inside Wyles' reach and pressed it to the man's throat.

"Stand down, fucker, or I'll slice you ear-to-ear."

* * * *

It didn't hurt. Aden knew he'd been slashed in various places, but he didn't feel any pain. Maybe that would come later. Now, all that mattered was protecting his underbelly from Pavel's kicking hind legs. He should have broken free to catch his breath, clear some of the stink of the wolverine's from his nostrils, and strategize his next move. But he wanted to end it and he knew that if he stopped, even for a second, his energy might flag. The wolverine wouldn't tire as easily. So, latching onto the familiar's throat, he wrapped all four legs around the stocky body and rolled them both toward the balustrade. He clenched his jaw as hard as he could and tasted blood. That gave him a burst of power that allowed him to spring free as soon as he felt them crash into the wood.

With the litheness of his kind, he jumped onto the railing and goaded the wolverine with a snarl. The beast responded with the blinding fury of his kind and lunged to meet Aden where he perched. Aden allowed Pavel to get one swipe in on his front leg before leaping into the air. As he twisted to land on his paws, he saw the wolverine, with his thick body, topple. No amount of scrambling could save him from the fall. He flew on his back, legs outstretched, before landing with a sickening thud.

Aden spared his enemy one long glance before bounding off to join his master.

* * * *

James tightened his grip on both the knife and Wyles' shoulders as the witch tried to force the blade from his hand.

"Stop it, you idiot. I'm right up against your jugular. If you keep trying to wrest it away from me, you'll be nicked and we both know you'll die within seconds." He hesitated. "Especially as I won't do a thing to try to stop you from bleeding out."

Wyles said nothing, but the force on the blade disappeared. They stood panting, both exhausted from the battle. James wasn't sure what his next move should be. And then it happened. He saw the wolverine through Aden's eyes, the connection between them flaring into place all of a sudden. The creature was falling through the air. He heard the beast's bones cracking and smelled the blood rising from the bottom of the inner courtyard.

He also felt Wyles deflate like a balloon, proof that he had been relying on his familiar's power for his strength.

"Your familiar is dead, Wyles. You've lost this battle, and the war, for that matter. I can expose you, but I still want to make a deal."

Wyles made a sound not unlike what his familiar must have sounded like. "You think this is over? My power is depleted, I'll give you that, but by morning I'll have had another familiar under me and formed a new bond. The Academy is always open if your pockets are deep enough. Maybe I'll pick a girl this time. Somebody pretty as well as formidable."

James wouldn't have thought he could be shocked easily, not with all that he'd seen in his relatively short life as a copper. But Wyles' lack of grief over the death of his familiar appalled him.

"You just lost the familiar who shared your life and your bed. He fought to the death for you. Is he so easily replaced in your mind?"

Wyles snorted. "You must be joking. Me, care about the death of a...tool? That thing meant no more to me than a paperweight. It served a purpose, although badly this night. I felt its despair as it died because it reached out to me. Disgusting. As if I cared for its feelings."

"It? Is that how you thought of your familiar?"

Wyles barked out a laugh. "Don't act so high and mighty about familiars. Yours is just a good fuck and a source of power to you too. You're no better than me."

No. The asshole was wrong. Aden meant more to him than pleasure and success. He *did*.

"James?"

"I'm fine. Stay away."

Wyles might be weak, but he was still dangerous. Even now, James dared not loosen his hold. "We're going to talk now, you and I, about the book."

Despite clear orders to the contrary, Aden came trotting into the office anyway.

James flexed his fingers to keep his grip on the knife tight. "Aden, I said to stay away. I'm handling Wyles. And" — he added when streaks of blood on the familiar's fur caused his heart to skip a beat — "you go lie down in the hall. Rest. I'll take care of you when I'm done here."

Aden stared at him with his beautiful green eyes, his distress a palpable thing. Then he turned to leave as commanded. A glass ashtray rose from the floor and headed toward the familiar's head. James didn't hesitate. He dug the blade into Wyles' neck and threw him to one side as far as he could. Blood sprayed as he did so, missing James, and Wyles made a gurgling sound. James didn't care. Wyles had signed his own death warrant the moment he chose to attack Aden. For all that it was the first time that he'd killed a man, James didn't spare him another glance. Instead, he focused on the ashtray dropping inches from Aden's head.

For a moment, time stopped. Or so it seemed. Neither he nor Aden moved or made any sort of sound as Wyles gasped his last. James couldn't hear his own breathing or heartbeat, nor that of his familiar, as he stared unblinking at an equally wide-eyed snow leopard. Then, with a lurch, James gasped and his pulse pounded inside his head as he dived toward Aden. He dropped to his knees and grabbed his familiar in a tight hug. He kissed the top of Aden's head, burying his face into the fur. The stench of the wolverine's scent glands assailed him, but he paid it no mind. Aden was alive. That was all that mattered.

"Oh, baby! Baby! Thank God you're alive." He pulled back at the feel of stickiness that had to be blood. "Shift for me. I want to see how hurt you are."

In the next instant, he was clasping warm flesh. Aden nestled closer to him and threw his arms around James' waist. Now the streaks of blood and the scratches causing it to well up were visible. James cupped Aden's chin and pulled it up so that they could look at one another.

"How bad is it, baby?"

"Not so bad. Everything is superficial. Shifting a few times will help." Aden ran his hands up James' arms, squeezing as he did so. "And you?" He glanced around. "It's like a war zone in here. Are you hurt?"

There were a few aches and pains from glancing blows that Wyles had managed to land with his flying objects, but he wasn't going to worry the boy with such trivialities. "I'm fine. Tired from so much cloaking," he admitted. "I need a moment to catch my breath before getting us out of here unseen."

And to hold you. Just hold you.

James indulged his need to give comfort to and get comfort from his familiar. The evening had nearly ended in disaster. If Aden hadn't prevailed...well, now he knew for sure what his feelings for the boy were. Aden was no tool to use and replace when needed. Once this horrid business was concluded, he would make sure to reveal his emotions and give them the name they deserved—love. At the same time, he believed even more firmly that keeping Aden and putting him in danger again was a selfish, *selfish* act. If he really loved the boy, he'd take him back to the Academy or, better yet, find him a decent, quiet witch, like a healer, to live with. The thought of someone else having Aden in their bed made his heart ache, but he had to at least try to do what was best for the familiar.

Knowing that if he stayed as he was for much longer he might never find the strength to press on with what needed to be done, he forced himself to his feet, letting go of Aden.

"I need you to shift now. I'll cloak us long enough to get out of this building unseen. There's no way we explain what happened here that won't end with me dangling from a rope." He winced at the look of horror crossing Aden's face.

"Won't people know anyway?" Fear laced Aden's question.

"No, don't worry. They won't. I doubt very much Wyles noted this meeting in his diary. He couldn't afford to answer any questions about why he was speaking with me after dark. And with both him and Pavel dead, there are no witnesses, other than those goons he hired. They'll be too scared of being accused of being my accomplices to say anything to anyone. And there isn't a soul around here, undoubtedly at Wyles' orders, to keep his secret.

"Come on now, shift."

Aden blinked once before standing on four paws. James wrapped the familiar in his cloaking shield and wasted no more time on Wyles. The man was dead and that was good enough for him. Once they were safely away, he'd have to make the decision of what to do next. He had considered this eventuality, although he'd hoped the man would see reason. There was really only one way left to keep Aden and himself safe.

* * * *

James grimaced at how his apartment looked pretty much the way Wyles' office had. His bully boys had done a fine job of searching for the ledger. "God, what a mess. No more than I expected, though." He shot Aden a reassuring smile.

In his human skin once more, the familiar showed fainter lines of scrapes and closed puncture wounds from teeth. Shifting did help with healing, but the evidence of the fight that he had forced his familiar in made his blood boil. It only served to make him even less concerned that he'd taken a life for the first time. Wyles had gotten what he'd deserved.

Aden took a step farther into the room. "I'll start cleaning up."

"No, you won't." James clasped Aden by the arm and pulled him over to the bed. "Sit. I'm going to draw you a bath. No argument," he added when Aden's mouth opened.

Obedient boy that he was, the familiar shut his lips in a firm line and nodded once. He wasn't happy about being pampered but that was too bad. It was the least James could do.

He ran a bath a bit shy of hot and added in some salts that smelled of lavender. Returning to the bed, he scooped Aden up into his arms to carry him to the tub.

"Hey, I can walk."

"I know you can, baby. Just let me do this for you, pamper you." He lowered the familiar into the water with as much care as he would a newborn and ran a hand over the boy's head. "You weren't supposed to get hurt. I thought—" He sighed heavily and hated how thick his voice became. "I thought having you there was insurance in case things got dicey, but I never thought you'd end up fighting for your life. Killing for it."

Aden lifted a hand to take James'. Fine lines of claw marks were now pink and not red. "I'm glad I was there to help you. And"—he moistened his lips—"taking Pavel doesn't bother me. I'm a leopard, remember? We're born to kill. You weren't, though. You cut Wyles' throat to protect me and I think it weighs heavily on you."

James brought Aden's hand to his lips and kissed the back of it. "I regret only underestimating Wyles' dedication to stopping me at all costs. His death won't haunt my dreams. Believe me. Now, rest and soak away your pains. Shift again if necessary and wait for me here. I'll be back as soon as I can."

"May I ask where you are going?"

James stopped at the door jamb and looked back. "To end this in the only way I know how."

* * * *

As James threw a third pebble at the upstairs window, he hoped like hell that he had the right room. Kitty was usually a light sleeper, yet no one responded, until the kitchen door suddenly opened and his grim-faced sister emerged to wave him in.

"For the love of suffering Jesus, what are you doing out here at this time of night?" Her voice, barely above a whisper, held the same withering tone that their mother's always did when vexed. And she tightened the belt of her robe with the same emphasis she'd learned at their mother's knee.

James didn't try to explain where others could hear. Instead, he meekly followed her back to her room and waited for her to shut the door before answering.

"I'm sorry. I need to take back the book."

Kitty huffed and went to pull it free from her stacks on the desk. She held it out to him. "It couldn't wait until morning?"

James clutched the thing to his chest, weariness washing over him. "No. I'm sorry but I didn't dare wait."

Kitty opened her mouth, then closed it again, and scrutinized his right shirt cuff. "Is that blood?" Her eyes went wide as she moved closer to look.

James backed away, annoyed with himself for not thinking to check if any of Wyles' blood had managed to hit despite his efforts to avoid it. "It's nothing."

His sister put her fists on her hips, apparently making a career out of mimicking their mother. "Don't be stupid. And don't act like *I* am. Are you all right? Is Aden?" Her concern for his familiar seemed even more pronounced than for him.

"I'm fine and so is he." His throat closed up with sudden emotion. "I put him in danger, Kitty. That poor boy was just looking for a witch to protect him and I put him in the middle of a vicious fight. He could have been killed." His voice broke and he had to turn away. His grip tightened on the hateful ledger that people were willing to do evil things to possess.

His sister came to put her arms around him from the back. "There now, I didn't mean to upset you. Aden's come through whatever it was and so have you. Don't fret."

James reined in his emotions. Or tried to. It was fatigue and the cooling of the blood after a fight that was making him want to weep. That was all. And yet... He kept picturing how Wyles had tried to smash his familiar's head in, unwilling to lose even then.

He took in a shuddering breath. "He's not merely a tool, you know."

"Aden, you mean?"

James nodded. "He's more than a means to an end, a power source easily replaced if I lose him."

"Well, of course he's not. He's a lovely boy, loyal and kind. I can see that. So can the Sisters. We all agree you got lucky finding him."

"I didn't *find* him, I bought him." He couldn't keep the bitterness out of his voice. The whole business had been sordid. He'd known it at the time, but had convinced himself that this was the natural way of the world and he would give the familiar a decent life while controlling the boy's natural aggressive urge. He couldn't ignore the ugliness of the rationalization now. Familiars were treated as slaves with the same justification that had always been used by those owning other people. He was disgusted with society for allowing it to continue, although no more so than he was at himself for going along with it.

Kitty rubbed her cheek against his back. "It's the way of things. You can't change that. You can only make a good life for him, and you are."

"Maybe I can't change the world, not on my own anyway. And I have soothed my own conscience by being as kind and generous with Aden as I can. I don't think I can hide behind that righteousness anymore, although the bond between Aden and me is strong. I must be doing something right. I don't have anything to compare it to, yet I think it's unusual." Even as he said the words out loud for the first time, he knew he was correct in his assumptions. Wyles' power had seemed weak compared to his own. And the moment the man had lost his familiar, he'd become easy to defeat. The only conceivable reason was that their bond, forced with no amount of respect or affection, had been perfunctory. He was sure of it now.

James turned to hug his sister properly. "I think I love him, Kitty. No, I *do* love him. Isn't that mad?"

"Not at all." She stood on tiptoes to kiss his cheek. "You've always been the best of us, Seamus Byrne. How could you not love someone who has given himself entirely to you? Go home to him and let him know your feelings."

He squeezed her for a second before letting go. "I will. First, though, I have to deal with this." He held up the ledger.

"What will you do?"

"Give it to the press."

Kitty frowned. "Is that wise? Can you not do some private deal to put this whole thing behind you?"

He held up his hand with the soiled cuff. "Tried that already. The only way to neuter those who seek this knowledge is to bring it to the public."

"Do you think what's in there will ever get out? You haven't told me much, but I'm sure the newspapers are in tight with politicians. You might be putting yourself in greater danger."

He nodded. "I've thought of that, but I've run out of options. There's a reporter that I trust. He'll find a way to get this information to print, in one way or another. Regardless, I've reached a point where the more people who know the same information as I do, the better for me. I'm nobody, after all."

"You're somebody to me. And to Aden, I'm sure. Stay safe, James."

"I will do my best. All I meant was that I'm not someone to worry about. Just a copper turned private detective. I'll give them bigger fish to fry." He leaned in to kiss her cheek. "Thanks for keeping this safe for me. I'll see you Sunday?"

"Hmm." Kitty rolled her eyes. "Ma insists I come over. Maybe Pa will be more accepting of my decision. I don't think so. It can't hurt to try for her sake, though."

"See, you're a good child. Better than I've been. Good night."

With that, James quietly let himself out of the house and headed for his next stop. He could only hope Mike would be as accepting about being awoken in the middle of the night. Given the news gold he held in his hand, James supposed the newsman would be quite forgiving.

Chapter Twelve

Aden looked around the apartment to see if he'd missed anything. That which could be righted, was. That which had been destroyed beyond repair sat in the dustbin. Fortunately, it wasn't overflowing. Wyles' goons had wrecked the place in search of a hiding spot for the damn book of sins, but they hadn't needed to break much and apparently hadn't been angry enough to bother to. It felt good to have done something productive while waiting for his witch to return. Lying in bed, trying to fall asleep and failing, had been a waste of time. Once he'd gotten up and started with the housekeeping, his nerves had calmed somewhat and the activity had allowed him to focus on something more than worry about where James was and if he were safe.

He went to the kitchen to brew some coffee. Footsteps sounded on the tread of the stairs. He shifted to be ready for a fight should trouble be coming. James' scent hit his leopard's nostrils almost at once. With relief, he shifted back into his human skin just as James was opening the door. The man didn't seem too happy to find Aden standing in front of him. He raised his eyebrows and shook his head as he closed the door behind him.

"You should be in bed, sleeping, baby."

Aden put his hands on his hips. "How was I supposed to do that with you out there on your own? I was worried." He dropped his gaze with a grimace.

James' hands cupped his face and lifted it. "I'm fine. Nobody was watching when I left, no one followed me, and no one is lingering across the street now. Wyles and Melinda must have been acting on their own. There's no vast conspiracy of Appleton's victims searching for Josie through us." He heaved a sigh. "I thought as much when I was talking to Wyles. It's good to know I was right."

James kissed him softly, slowly, then lifted his lips away in order to hug Aden close.

Aden melted into the embrace and wrapped his arms around the man's waist. "Is it done, then?"

"Almost. We need to fetch Josie this morning and let him know what's happened. He'll have to make a decision about what to do next."

Their bodies reacted in what he now knew was a predictable way when two men who wanted each other touched. Because he was naked, Aden's erection was the more obvious one. He couldn't help rubbing against the raspy cloth of James' trousers.

The witch chuckled. "I can tell how happy you are for me to be home again."

"I'm always happy when I'm with you."

"I feel the same, but I'm sorry to say I'm exhausted. I need a few hours of sleep before we head over to the rectory." He yawned loudly and tugged Aden toward the bed. "Lie down with me. You must be exhausted too."

"Not so much." Aden allowed himself to be led. "We familiars get a lot out of shifting. My energy hasn't flagged, although my human half could use some sleep. Not much."

When they reached the side of the bed, Aden didn't allow James to pull him down. Instead, he wiggled from the man's embrace and began to help him disrobe. He took the jacket James had already started to remove and hung it up in the closet before removing the man's pocket watch and placing it carefully on the nightstand. Then he knelt down between the witch's legs and brushed aside his hands to get the boots off himself. Next, he reached up to undo the buttons of the waistcoat and the shirt. He pulled off the collars and cuffs and took all of it to the closet. He frowned when he caught sight of a bit of blood and put it aside to try to clean later. By the time he turned back, James was undoing his trousers, a sexy grin on his face.

"Eager to get me naked, are you, baby?"

Aden rolled his eyes. "Always. You've created a monster in me. More than I already was, of course."

James' eyes turned hard. "Never say that about yourself. You are not a monster. You are a lovely boy who happens to have the added gift of turning into a fierce creature." James looked as if he wanted to say more, then shook his head and lay on his back. "Help me with this last bit, will you?"

"Certainly."

Pleased to be of service even in this small way with James' blessing, he tugged the trousers off the man's leg, leaving him in his union suit and socks. The half-hard cock tented the soft linen. It would be so easy to wiggle his fingers past the cloth and clasp the shaft. His own dick twitched with encouragement. But James' eyes were already closed. So, Aden simply lifted his witch's big legs onto the bed, maneuvered his head onto the pillow and spread the coverlet over his body. By the time Aden slid in beside him, James was breathing with the heaviness of sleep.

Now that his witch was safely back with him, Aden closed his eyes to do the same.

* * * *

Aden woke to a hot embrace with rock-hard arms wrapped tightly around him. Something else that was hot and hard pressed into his ass cheeks, seeking, probing and begging entrance. He gave his permission by pushing back to allow James' dick to breach his hole. The quick burn of being stretched, so familiar to him now after such a short time, only served to heighten his own arousal. His dick and balls ached with a need that hadn't abated since he'd gone to sleep. Instead, it had invaded his dreams, goading him to action. He moaned and arched his back.

James didn't require much encouragement. His palm flattened against Aden's abdomen and pushed him onto the cock while James' hips snapped into a thrust that buried the witch's dick deep inside Aden's channel. James threw his leg over Aden's to press them even closer together. He stopped moving and simply let his cock pulse within Aden's ass.

"Sorry, baby. I had to have you. Just…had to get inside you as far as I could."

Aden shuddered out a breath and squeezed the shaft with his sphincter. "I'm not complaining. I love the feel of you, filling me, claiming me. I love *you*, James."

The man gave a choked gasp, his warm breath tickling Aden's ear. "I don't understand how. I nearly got you killed."

"No. I was always going to win against that wolverine. I'm a snow leopard. You picked me for my fierceness."

James tightened his arms. "I picked you because you were and are the most beautiful creature I've ever seen. I've never wanted to bed a man, but I wanted you with a strength of desire that frightened me. It still does."

Warmth spread through him. It wasn't the declaration of love that he might have hoped for, but knowing that his witch wanted him so very much was the next best thing. "Show me," he dared to say.

After a second of hesitation, the man did just that. He pressed Aden onto his stomach and braced his arms on either side of Aden's head. And he began to thrust. Slowly and shallowly at first, then with increased speed and depth. The witch rolled his hips with each push inward, scraping against that sensitive spot within Aden that caused his balls to tingle and his arousal to climb. Aden moaned and clenched the sheets, using the grip to hump himself against the mattress.

"That's my job." James tucked one arm around Aden's waist and lifted him just enough to get his fingers around Aden's shaft. That small amount of movement also sent James' dick farther inside Aden's ass.

Aden mewled. "Faster, James. Harder."

His witch gave him everything he demanded, driving into him while jerking his shaft with a hard grip. Aden cried out as the orgasm ripped through him. He clenched his fingers and squinted his eyes tightly shut until he saw stars. His breath tore out of him in ragged pants. He bucked as if he needed to throw his man off, even as he squeezed to keep him inside.

With a bellow, James came too, his cum coating Aden's channel, easing the burn of his thrusts. Aden wanted that bite of pain back, but there was no keeping his witch inside. When the last of his spurts came out, so did James. The man eased out of Aden and rolled them both so that Aden lay on James' chest.

"Baby." James peppered him with kisses. "I didn't hurt you, did I?"

"No. Couldn't you tell how hard I came?" Even now, Aden's heart beat a rapid tattoo and his breath was labored.

James carded his fingers through Aden's damp hair. "Pleasure and pain often go together. I don't want to ever tip the scales so that it's too much of the latter."

"Never." He wanted to once again declare his love for his witch, yet didn't dare. Saying it too much when James couldn't return the sentiment would only make the guy feel bad. Or annoyed. Aden didn't want to risk eliciting either feeling. It was enough that his witch truly wanted him and wasn't merely tolerating him for the power he gave.

They lay in a sweaty tangle of limbs. Dawn had already crept past the curtains. They'd have to get up and finish this business with Josie. Aden wondered what work James would get after this. And as much as he trusted James' judgment, he worried that this problem hadn't been solved and that they were still in danger.

He dared to voice some of his concerns in the form of a question. "What happened when you left here last night? Did you get the book from Kitty?"

"Yes. And then I went round to my newspaper friend Mike's house." He chuckled. "His missus wasn't pleased by that, I can tell you."

Aden levered up on his elbows to look at James. "Is he going to publish the information in there?"

James shrugged and played with some strands of Aden's hair. "I don't know. I hope so. He certainly wants to. He was practically salivating as he skimmed the thing in front of me. But he's not in charge of those decisions and his editor and publisher might very well find friends of theirs inside those pages. Even if they don't, they'd be making a lot of powerful enemies."

"But...it's a newspaper. Aren't they supposed to print the truth, not cover it up?"

"Oh, baby. I wish the world weren't such a shitty place that what you say would always be true. I simply don't know. Mike was keen, as I said, and I can tell you that and he's no fool, so he's not going to keep it to himself. The more people who know about it, the safer we all are. A cover-up only works if you can contain the people who know about it.

"We'll see. The good news is that we are in the clear. As is Josie. Melinda will learn of Wyles' death soon enough, if not by word of mouth then in the paper. I'm sure the nightguard will eventually find both bodies, and the story will likely be out this morning no matter how quiet the mayor or anyone else tries to keep it. In any event, I'll make sure Mrs. Appleton knows the book is out of ours and Josie's hands. She'll have to find another way to keep her lifestyle once her husband dies."

James sat up, taking Aden with him so that he straddled the man's hips. He stroked a finger down Aden's cheek, keeping his gaze fixed on Aden's eyes. Then he kissed him long and slowly, his tongue doing a lazy sweep of Aden's mouth. When he pulled back, Aden tried to follow for more, but James held him back.

Aden smiled. "What? You want me again. I can feel it." The witch's cock was starting to thicken, as was Aden's.

"I want you always, baby. Never doubt that." He glanced down for a moment before returning to look intensely into Aden's eyes. "It's not only the sex and the power that comes with it." He tucked strands of hair behind Aden's ear before cupping his face. "You've said you love me a few times now."

Aden's breath caught. "I'm sorry. I won't say it again if it bothers you."

James shook his head. "I'm doing a terrible job of this. What I'm trying to say is that hearing it the first time made me stop and think about what our relationship was truly turning out to be. I needed time to sort my own feelings, but after fearing for your life, knowing that you killed for me, I've seen deep into my own heart."

Aden dared not hope that he was going to hear what he desperately wanted to. After the intense night they'd had, he didn't want James to say anything he might regret. "It's all right," he interjected. "Killing isn't the same for familiars as it might be for humans, especially predators like me. I have not an ounce of guilt over what I did, especially as it was to protect you."

James pressed their foreheads together. "I appreciate what you're saying, baby. And for the record, I won't lose a moment of sleep over killing

Wyles to protect you." He sighed heavily. "I really do wish I were better at revealing my feelings because what I'm trying to say is that I love you, too."

Aden's breath caught and his heart skipped a hard beat hearing his witch declare his love. He wanted this so much, yet didn't want James to speak words he might regret. "I'm so very glad, James. I really am. I'll understand, though, if you don't quite mean it later after this mess is done with."

James glared and gave him a little shake. "You think this is in the heat of the moment? That I'll regret telling you I love you? You couldn't be more wrong." He glanced away and licked his lips. "You know when Wyles and I were doing the dance of the flying objects in his office, he was very chatty. He didn't care anything about Pavel, only about Pavel losing and putting him at a disadvantage. He was already contemplating having to replace him and said it was easy. That the Academy was full of familiars he could buy and exploit. Pavel was nothing more than a *tool* for him.

"As I listened to what he said, I realized that I didn't see you like that. I never had, although when I walked into the Academy, I really kind of thought the same thing—I'll just find a familiar who can help my business and will be good enough to bed. The second I laid eyes on you, the kernel of love I have lodged in my heart started to take root. I just didn't realize it at the time."

Aden's brain froze. He couldn't think of a single word to express the joy in him at hearing those words. James didn't give him a chance to respond in any event because the man followed up with words that froze Aden's blood.

"And because I do love you and I realize now that the way witches find their familiars isn't fair to the familiars, I have to once again give you the choice of whether to stay with me or not. It would be better for you if you left me."

Aden pulled away. "You don't want me!"

The man grabbed him into a deep and arousing kiss, then tugged him off the bed. "Of course I want you! What part of my saying I love you made you think the opposite? I just can't force you to stay. It's not right. I see that now. Being together has to be your choice, too. And I also want what's best for you. That's part of love, Aden — putting the interests of the other person before your own."

"How could you think for a second that I want to be with anyone else? Do you think I'm telling you what I think you'd like to hear? Because I'm not. Revealing my love for you was both the most natural thing in the world and the scariest. I was taught to keep such thoughts to myself, but couldn't keep back my feelings. I love you, James, not because I have to but because you are the most wonderful witch in the world. I will have no other." Aden frowned and nodded firmly to convey his resolve.

James let out a shuddering sigh. "Thank God. I was trying to do right by you even though I was scared you might want to leave. I've caused you nothing except trouble so far."

"Let's not talk about that again. Please. Fighting for you gave me great joy. It's what I'm born to do. I am your familiar, James Byrne, for the rest of our lives."

"You humble me. And I promise I'll get this whole horrible business sorted today."

They were both hard and Aden dug in his heels to stay where they were when James pulled him toward the bathroom. "Take me back to bed. Make us both happy. Please?"

James shook his head and jutted his chin toward the window. "The morning has started, baby. We need to get to the rectory. That doesn't mean we can't jerk each other off while we bathe. I'm afraid if we lie down again, I may never get up."

With that, James took hold of Aden's dick and led him laughing into the bathroom.

* * * *

"Good morning, Father Mark."

James was very chipper as he greeted the priest at the back door of the rectory. Aden sat on his haunches, on the alert for trouble, his tail twitching. Because they had motored over and room was needed for Josie when they left again, James had decided it would be best for Aden to shift for the whole journey. Aden didn't mind. He was worried trouble still lurked and he would be better able to protect his witch this way.

Father Mark waved them in, a napkin in one hand. "Good timing, James. The housekeeper will be here within the hour. My guest is finishing his breakfast but otherwise ready to go. It seems your troubles might be over?"

The priest raised his eyebrows as he returned to his seat at the kitchen table, where Josie also sat reading the paper. The young man grinned broadly at them.

"Have you seen the morning paper?" Josie slapped it front page up on the table and pointed to the headline. "Someone did the odious Mr. Wyles in.

They're saying that he was a witch and that his assistant was a familiar. A wolverine! And found smashed from a fall in the inner rotunda. I wonder what happened to him?" Josie's eyes widened.

James barely glanced at the paper. "It can be hard to detect a witch if he's keen on hiding it. There were rumors about Wyles, I heard, that included his cheating at gambling. It's possible those sins caught up to him. I bet the mayor didn't know a thing about it."

Josie blinked a few times rapidly. "Really? So the mayor wasn't in the book, after all?"

James shook his head. "No, I don't believe so."

"Ah, well, that's a relief, actually. I rather like the man, myself," Father Mark said. "I didn't know Mr. Wyles, but gambling is indeed a sin and cheating at it even worse. I'm not sure that warrants a man's death, however." He looked pointedly at James from over the rim of his teacup.

"Perhaps fighting to the death was his choice even when offered another way out. And, of course, his familiar was always going to go the way his master dictated. There might not have been any way to avoid such a fight, and, if so, maybe the better man came out victorious." James laid a comforting hand on Aden's head, petting him.

"I can believe that." Father Mark stood. "Now, if you'll excuse me, I must get to church." He smiled at Josie. "Goodbye to you. You've been an excellent guest and I wish you well."

"Thank you, Father. I can't tell you how much I appreciate your hospitality."

The priest pointed upward. "My boss would tolerate no less."

With that, the man left. Josie stood to clear the table of his dishes, wash them and put them away with obviously practiced efficiency. "It wouldn't do for Mrs. Flanagan to think Father Mark has been harboring a guest." He turned and leaned against the counter. "What now?"

"After Wyles proved…intractable, I gave the book to my reporter friend. I don't know what will happen with the information contained within it but, now that it's in another's hands, Melinda has no reason to come after you. That's assuming she could find someone to replace Wyles in aiding her effort."

"So, I'm free?" The hopefulness in the man's voice made Aden proud to have played a part in putting it there.

"As soon as we make sure Melinda has gotten the message, yes."

Josie made a face. "You mean you want me to go tell her?"

"I mean, we'll all go. Let's put this whole thing to bed and leave your father and stepmother to stew in their own juices."

* * * *

The rush of air in James' face blew away the fatigue that kept threatening to knock him on his ass. It wouldn't be long now before he could take his familiar home and crawl back into bed. First to sleep, then…well, they were doing pretty well in that department in such a very short time. It lifted his spirits to know not only that was his first case nearly done but that he was partnered up with someone that he loved and enjoyed. And *partner* was the right word for Aden.

He couldn't understand how other witches could keep an emotional distance from their familiar or treat them at best like pets instead of human beings. No matter that Aden sat curled in Josie's embrace in leopard form—underneath that fur was a man. He deserved as much dignity and respect as any other.

This visit with Mr. and Mrs. Appleton shouldn't take long. He'd make sure Melinda at least understood there was nothing to be gained by chasing after Josie. If she were smart, she'd be making plans right that morning to escape the bricks that were poised to tumble down on their heads. He wasn't sure whether to be disappointed on Josie's behalf or not when he pulled up to the house on Louisburg Square and saw the black wreath hanging on the door.

He cut the motor and grimaced at his passenger. "I'm sorry. I doubt the house is in mourning over Wyles."

Josie shrugged. "When my father kicked me out of the house, he said he hoped that when some other deviant inevitably cut my throat, they'd at least have the decency to dispose of me somewhere my body wouldn't be found to embarrass him." He looked at the door, then at James. "I can't say I feel any grief over this. Please don't worry about that."

James expected they'd run into trouble getting admitted to the house, but Josie solved that potential problem by simply opening the door. He stepped into the marble foyer just as an older man neatly dressed in livery came from an archway.

"Master Josiah. Welcome home. We didn't know how to contact you to deliver the sad news."

Josie waved the comment away. "Not to worry, Jenson. I wasn't readily available and I actually have only learned of my father's passing because of the mourning wreath. It is he who's dead, isn't it?"

"Of course it's your father, you stupid, selfish boy." Melinda's voice floated down from the staircase as she descended dressed in bombazine widow's weeds that somehow enhanced her beauty. She certainly didn't have eyes puffy from weeping. "That will be all, Jenson."

When it was only the four of them left, she walked right up to Josie and raised her hand. Before she was close enough to deliver the slap she so obviously intended, Aden leapt between them and hissed. That brought the woman up short.

"Control your beast, you filthy Irishman."

James bared his teeth. "He controls himself, don't you know." Nevertheless, he drew Josie farther away from her and was pleased when Aden followed. "I'd offer my condolences on your loss, but I'm too tired to pretend either of us cares."

"Then why are you here? When the mayor hears about this…this invasion of my home, you'll be run out of town."

"And just who is going to tell him? Wyles? Have you seen the morning paper, Mrs. Appleton? Mr. Wyles got himself into a spot of trouble. He's not going to be able to tell anyone anything ever again."

Understanding slowly entered her eyes. "What have you done?"

"Nothing. Oh, except I gave the book to a reporter. Neither Josie nor I have it anymore, and the tales inside it are for someone else to tell. I'm not sure you'll have many friends left once word about your husband's true business gets out."

The woman's eyes flashed with fury, although there was a hint of fear in them as well. "No one would dare print a word of it. I have powerful people on my side."

James inclined his head. "I'm sure there are powerful people who want to protect themselves. I doubt any of them will give a rat's ass about you, Mrs. Appleton."

The woman's face turned bright red, but a warning growl from Aden stopped her from doing anything rash. She turned to spew her venom on Josie. "You won't get a penny of his estate."

"Save it for the lawyers I bet you'll need when people believe you were part of the blackmail. I don't want any of his dirty money. I never did. You should have left me alone, Melinda. You and Wyles wouldn't have been able to squeeze people for more money, but you wouldn't have been exposed, either. Your stupidity and greed exceeded even my expectations. Goodbye."

Josie turned on his heels and strode out of the house without a backward look, leaving Melinda sputtering with rage.

"What he said." James couldn't help giving the dig, then followed Josie out with Aden at his side. The air on the street smelled cleaner than that in the house. He took a deep breath and let it out with relief. "Where to now, Josie?"

"Freaktown, of course. It's a nicer part of Boston than this place will ever be."

Epilogue

James threw himself onto the bed, fully clothed, the moment he and Aden returned to their apartment. The rumpled sheets held the scent of how they'd spent the first few minutes of the day. The mere thought of it set his dick to trying to rally. It didn't quite get where it needed to be, exhaustion rolling over him and damping all other sensations. Even when Aden shifted and stood gloriously naked in front of him, he still didn't think he could perform to either of their satisfactions. Better to sleep for a few hours, then spend the rest of the day in bed. Maybe he'd take Aden out to dinner later, though. He bet the boy had never eaten in a restaurant and, as fine as he looked in the real suit James had ordered for him, James would be proud to been seen with him.

He held out his hand. "Come and lie down. We've had a hell of a few days. With Josie back where he belongs, I can't wait to put this whole miserable thing behind us. We both need sleep, then food."

James struggled out of his suit coat so it wouldn't be wrinkled and smelly later. He was delighted when Aden helped him undress, tackling his boots first. Soon he wore only his union suit. The outline of his thickening cock was visible through the thin material. Aden's hungry gaze at it almost was enough to make him fully hard. With a groan of disappointment at his own limitations, he pulled the familiar down to his side.

"As tempting as you are, baby, I need some sleep before I can mount you again. I can see you have no trouble. Then again, you are younger." *Almost too young.*

He snuggled with his familiar in his arms. Yet, as tired as he was, he couldn't quite shut off his brain. Thoughts kept nagging at him. He'd declared his love to Aden and had no doubts about his feelings. There was more, however, that needed to be said and done, he realized. Until he addressed that, he wasn't going to be able to truly relax.

Hugging Aden closer, he spoke in a low tone in the boy's ear. "What is your last name?"

"*Byrne.*" There was an amused tone in his voice.

"No, I mean before you came home with me. I know the convention is for a familiar to become one with the witch legally, including taking their name. But I'm not comfortable with that. I mean, you're your own person, Aden. You should have your own identity."

"Oh." Aden was quiet for a few seconds. "I don't want the last name I had at birth. My parents gave me to the Academy and from that moment forward, I was no longer part of their family. They disowned me. Their name isn't mine anymore."

"Jesus wept." James understood all of this. It still broke his heart. How could anyone not love Aden? He kissed the boy's temple. "Pick another one, then. Something you like. Something meaningful to you. Take your time, baby. We have lots of it now."

Satisfied that he'd gotten the last thing off his chest, he started to drift off, Aden soft and warm against him. He had no idea what the next day would bring. It was possible no other clients would present themselves any time soon. Maybe that was okay. This first case had been more than he'd bargained for.

They'd be all right, though, he and Aden. He'd make sure of it.

* * * *

James had surprised Aden by not returning right away to the office. Instead, he'd taken Aden around the city, showing him the sights, pampering him with food and more clothing. No amount of objection was tolerated. James insisted that Aden had earned the time off. They had enough money to take it easy, James had assured him. And since that was the witch's duty to worry over, Aden allowed himself to simply enjoy spending lazy days with his loving witch. They even went to see Josie at his new job playing the piano in Freaktown. It was another all-male establishment, so James was open in his affection. Aden basked in it.

But it was time to get back to work. As they approached the building where the office was located, James stopped and pointed up. "Look, baby. I had a new sign erected."

Aden tipped his head and had to blink. He couldn't believe what he saw. *Raven and Snow Detective Agency,*

Seeker Witch and Familiar. After sleeping on it just once, the answer to James' question about what Aden wanted for a last name become obvious. He was a snow leopard, so Snow was the best name for him.

He turned to James with wide eyes. "You put me on the sign?"

"Of course. We're partners." He pecked Aden on the nose. "I want the world to know it's you and me, working together. And what a hell of a team we make, huh?"

Slinging his arm around Aden's shoulders, James walked them in and up the stairs to the office. They hadn't been back since that first day when Melinda Appleton blew into their lives. It was musty, so James opened a window.

"It's a nice day. Let's get some fresh air in here, shall we?"

Aden smiled. "Yes." He looked around. "Do you mind if I shift and lie on the window seat?"

"Whatever you want, partner. This is our place to do with as we wish."

Aden carefully removed his suit and put everything away in the closet. Then he shifted and bounded over to the window. He turned and kneaded the cushion until he had the perfect place to lie down. He put his head on his paws and looked over at James.

The man sat in his big chair behind the desk. "Well, now. We wait to see what comes next. Even though we don't appear in Mike's story about the blackmail, I feel certain word will get around to the right people that we were involved in some fashion. If nothing else, those who attended the party will remember us. *You,* really. It's just a matter of time before another client comes through that door."

Aden hoped so. For the time being, he was going to lie in the sun and bask in the warmth of it and the love he'd found in his life.

Sign up for our newsletter and find out about all our romance book releases, eBook sales and promotions, sneak peeks and FREE romance books!

Want to see more from this author?
Here's a taster for you to enjoy!

Raven and Snow:
Chasing His Dream
Samantha Cayto

Coming 2026

Excerpt

James Byrne, former cop and seeker witch, loved Boston. He really did. It was a small, yet bustling city, poised at the edge of the Atlantic Ocean that experienced all the weather that God and Mother Nature had to offer. Each of the four seasons had unique characteristics to recommend them. And James appreciated all of them — the cool crispness of fall with its gorgeous riot of leaf color, the snow and ice of winter for sledding and ice skating on Frog Pond, the fresh start that was spring exploding with renewed life and the growing warmth of summer that compelled people to spend a day frolicking at the beach. He couldn't imagine living anywhere that was endlessly cold or hot, sunny or overcast. How boring.

He reminded himself of all this as he sat sweltering in his office. Even with the window open and the luxury of the ceiling fan rotating above his head, there was no relief from the relentless heat of August. It was hot enough that he sat in his shirtsleeves. Very unprofessional, but it wasn't as if he expected any visitors. After his early triumph of thwarting the would-be blackmailer, Wyles, his detective agency hadn't seen people knocking down the doors for his services. Oh, he had collected small fees for finding lost items, but his hopes of the high-class Boston residents coming to him for serious help had been dashed. And the money that Melinda Appleton had showered him with to buy his complicity in her schemes had been spent. His pay-out from the police force was likewise nearly gone. He wasn't sure how long he'd be able to afford his office or his precious automobile. Times were *tight*.

James wadded up another page of the newspaper and tossed it into his wastepaper basket a few feet from his desk. As timewasters went, the game was as good as any. He didn't have to expend a lot of energy and he took a pathetic amount of pride in his aim getting better. There weren't many pages left, however, to turn into mini basketballs. And it was getting time to think about closing up that which didn't need to be open in the first place, sadly, and figuring out what he was going to do about supper. There wasn't much money in his pocket at the moment. Still, it wasn't only his hunger he had to assuage, so he needed to be creative in his purchases. He glanced over to the corner where Aden lay curled up in the coolest darkness the room had to offer. Snow leopards weren't meant for hot and steamy climates and the boy didn't seem to be any more comfortable in his human skin. At least in animal form, he could pant some of the heat out of his body.

This was what kept James up at night. He wasn't responsible for only himself anymore. His familiar counted on him to provide food and shelter and everything else that people needed to survive. James was becoming sick with worry that he wouldn't be able to take proper care of the boy. Not that Aden ever complained about or demanded anything. No, he accepted whatever James gave him, however meager, with sincere appreciation. That didn't change the fact that James wanted to give him far more because the boy had known little but cold duty from first his parents, then the familiar academy where they'd dumped him out of fear and a certain amount of greed, no doubt. Plus, he loved the boy with greater and more frightening depth each passing day. It was simply inconceivable that he would fail in giving Aden the best life possible.

He slipped his pocket watch out of his vest and looked at the time. Three in the afternoon, sufficiently late in the day to give up on anything happening. They could grab a sandwich from a street vendor and find a big, shady tree in the Common to relax and eat under until the sun went down and the heat dissipated as much as it was going to. The apartment would be as hot as the office, if not hotter, and with no fan to help stir the air. There was no reason to go there any sooner than was necessary.

James rose from his chair, gathered all the paper balls that hadn't landed in the basket, then slipped on his jacket. God, even the light linen material made him feel as if he'd just draped himself in hot water bottles. He hoped he would live long enough to see the day when people could walk around with fewer clothes without being arrested for indecency. Of course, he could go to the beach and put on his bathing suit, but that would mean exposing Aden to even more of the sun and there hadn't been time or money to buy such a limited type of clothing for the boy. He wasn't going to torture his familiar to get some relief for himself.

Damn it!

He was about to rouse Aden when hurried footsteps caught his attention. Someone was coming at a rush, which gave James his first real hope in weeks. Nothing caused that much urgency unless it was very important. And really, that could merely mean a beloved pet was missing and not a stolen jewel of great value or the wayward scion of a wealthy family. That type of low-level work wouldn't cover more than a few days of sandwiches, if that. Even as he faced the door, he braced for disappointment.

The door burst open to reveal a tall, whip-thin man with wide eyes and ginger hair sticking up in wild fashion as if his fingers had been pulling on it for hours. Although dressed as a gentleman, he was clearly not wealthy as the fashion of the garments was outdated and his cuffs were visibly frayed. Nevertheless, James straightened and put on his best smile. From his place in the corner, Aden opened his eyes.

The visitor marched up to the desk. "Mr. Byrne? Or, are you Mr. Snow?" The man's voice was reedy and his accent wasn't local.

"I'm James Byrne, seeker witch." He gestured toward Aden. "That is my familiar and partner, Mr. Snow."

The man whipped his long face in Aden's direction. His eyes widened a bit. "Oh, er, yes, I see." He returned his stare to James, his prominent Adam's apple bobbing on a hard swallow. Then he plucked at his collar and clutched a brown satchel, not unlike James', tightly to his chest.

When nothing more was forthcoming, James took up the reins of conversation. "Please sit." He gestured to his one visitor chair before plopping his ass on his own. He waited a few seconds before asking, "How may we help you, Mr....?"

More tugging and swallowing. "It's professor. I'm Professor Horace Bullwinkle."

Of course you are. James hadn't met any academics that he could recall, but this man met his expectations of what one looked like. Once again, he waited in vain for more information.

James softly cleared his throat. "What do you need us to find, Professor Bullwinkle?"

"Oh, um. A book? Yes, a book," he amended his question to a statement.

James' heart sank. He would have preferred to find another cat. This man certainly looked like someone who would have one as a pet. Still, work was work. He steepled his fingers on his desk blotter and called upon his limited patience.

"What kind of book, Professor?"

A line of sweat trickled down the man's temple, although whether it was from exertion in this heat or nervousness, one couldn't tell. "Forgive me, Mr. Byrne, but do you need to know that information in order to find it?"

James immediately became suspicious even though the man sitting in front of him looked like someone who would forget to eat until he passed out from hunger. So, he kept his voice calm and his expression non-threatening as he answered.

"I'm afraid I do, yes. It helps me focus my powers and be able to confirm that I've found the right one when I locate it." This was mostly true, although he wanted to tease out of his maybe-client that which he was obviously hiding. The last thing James and Aden needed was another Josie Appleton situation.

The professor's gaze dropped. "Yes, of course. I really should have known that because..." He sat up straighter. "I'm a witch myself."

That was interesting information. Normally, as a witch, James had no trouble knowing another of his kind when he met one. This guy was very adept at hiding his nature. The question was why? In the next second he had his answer.

"You see, Mr. Byrne, I'm a very religious person and believe that the, um, witch part of me is a test of my faith. I refuse to give into it. Not that I condemn others for doing so, mind you. No offense intended."

James flashed a grin. "No, of course not." Just another hypocrite, frowning on others until they needed something for themselves. "What is this book?" He prompted because really, Bullwinkle wasn't the only one sweating. James wanted out of the office as soon as possible.

The professor's gaze skidded away. "This is so embarrassing."

"I assure you we're very discreet. No one will ever know you sought out the services of a witch."

Bullwinkle shook his head. "That's not it. My chagrin comes from having to confess to you that I did something quite beyond the bounds of propriety."

"Is this an indecent book of some sort? Perhaps one with pictures of scantily clad ladies?" As he asked the question, he wondered why someone would take the trouble to find such a thing. Unless the man had been stupid enough to pen in his name or something.

Bullwinkle's chin kicked up. "Certainly not! I'm a religious man, as I've said. The book itself is perfectly respectable. A history of ancient Egypt, as it happens. It's a centuries-old copy of the much older text of an Egyptian priest."

"So, it's valuable." James was beginning to warm up to this engagement.

"For a scholar such as myself, it's priceless."

And there went his burgeoning excitement.

"Look, Professor, I don't mean to be rude, but I really must insist you explain what is going on."

The man appeared chastened. "Of course. My apologies." He leaned forward, that satchel still clutched to his breast as if it were his child. "I'm a professor of history at Harvard. Ancient Egypt is my specialized area. I've even had the privilege of being on a dig myself some years ago. It was the most amazing experience." His eyes lit up briefly with an almost fervor. "It is also my great fortune that I have access to reference material at the university's library. Such a rich resource. But also one that comes with strict rules. One of which is that one may not take certain books *out* of the library."

James glanced pointedly at the satchel. "Can I assume you broke that rule?"

"Sadly, yes." Bullwinkle patted his satchel. "I always have this with me. I'm very careful not to let it out of my sight, and I had only just found this magnificent book, hidden away, forgotten by my colleagues. There wasn't a lot of time to read it, then the library was closing for the day. I just couldn't wait a whole night to get it in my hands again. Nothing was going to happen to it. Nothing was supposed to, anyway. Somewhere, somehow between my leaving the campus and journeying to my home in Cambridge, it simply...disappeared. I'll lose my job if they find out." He added in a low voice, "To say nothing of having lost a valuable resource in my field."

When the man once more went silent on him, James took a piece of foolscap, his pen and inkwell and slid them over to the edge of the desk along with his blotter. "Professor, I need you to please write down everywhere you went and everything you did that day after leaving the library. And it would be helpful if you had something connected to the book that I can use as a talisman for it. Although, being a reference book, I assume there is nothing."

Bullwinkle had been reaching for the pen. Instead, he opened his satchel. "Oh, but there is something." He handed over a worn leather bookmark. "I used this, as I always do. For whatever reason, it was left behind by whom I can only assume was a thief." The professor proceeded in scratching out words on the paper.

James took the item and rubbed the soft material with his forefinger and thumb. There was something there, faint, yet distinct. And not in a good way. He supposed it echoed the many people who had touched the book over the centuries, some good, some not so much.

He placed it on his desk and reached for the piece of paper. "With these two things, I should be able to locate it." He scanned the information the professor had provided. There wasn't much, but it gave him a path to tread and hopefully that would strengthen what he felt from the bookmark.

The professor breathed out heavily. "Thank the Lord. I didn't know where to turn for help and keep this horrible affair quiet." He stood and reached into his coat pocket to take out a fairly—and surprisingly—thick money clip. "Will this be enough to cover your fee?" the man asked as he handed over twice as much as James had intended to charge.

Tempting as it was, he didn't take the whole of it. He stood to take the wad of cash, then peeled off the right amount. "This will do, thank you."

Bullwinkle stuffed the returned money and the clip back into his pocket. "You're too kind." He licked his lower lip. "May I ask when you'll get started? I'm not the only person who might request this particular book and when the librarian can't find it…"

"I understand, Professor. We'll get started right away. If all goes well, we might have it back to you tonight."

"Oh, that would be wonderful." Gratitude showed in the man's eyes.

"No promises, but we'll do our best. Where can we find you once we have the book?"

Bullwinkle rattled off his address. "You'll find me there. I rarely go out and won't leave my home unless it's to teach. Or eat. I do need to do that." He frowned, as if taking the time to put food in his belly was an inconvenience.

No hand was offered as the professor turned toward the door, and James sensed that a gentlemanly shake was not something Bullwinkle would welcome, so James stayed behind the desk.

Bullwinkle paused on his way out and he stared at Aden. The familiar had remained awake, listening as always, yet had made no noise to call attention to himself. James couldn't wait to hear the boy's take on this new client of theirs. The familiar had a keen sense when it came to humans. James' trusted his judgment completely.

The professor looked at James over his shoulder. "Such a lovely creature. I've always liked cats. The Egyptians worshipped them, you know." The same intensity as before flashed in his eyes. Then with that confession made, the man left.

About the Author

Samantha Cayto is a Boston-area native who practices as a business lawyer by day while writing erotic romance at night—the steamier the better. She likes to push the envelope when it comes to writing about passion and is delighted other women agree that guy-on-guy sex is the hottest ever.

She lives a typical suburban life with her husband, three kids and four dogs. Her children don't understand why they can't read what she writes, but her husband is always willing to lend her a hand—and anything else—when she needs to choreograph a scene.

Samantha loves to hear from readers. You can find her contact information, website details and author profile page at https://www.firstforromance.com

ENTWINED PUBLISHING